Bad to the Bone

by Danny Campbell
and Kimberly Campbell

Illustrated by Ray daSilva

Bad to the Bone is hand-illustrated by the same Grade A Quality Jumbo artists who bring you *Disney's Doug*, the television series.

New York

Original characters for "The Funnies" developed by
Jim Jinkins and Joe Aaron.

Printed in the United States of America

First Edition

1 3 5 7 9 10 8 6 4 2

The artwork for this book was prepared using pen and ink.

The text for this book is set in 13-point Leewood.

Library of Congress Catalog Card Number: 00-101763

ISBN 0-7868-4412-4

For more Disney Press fun, visit www.disneybooks.com

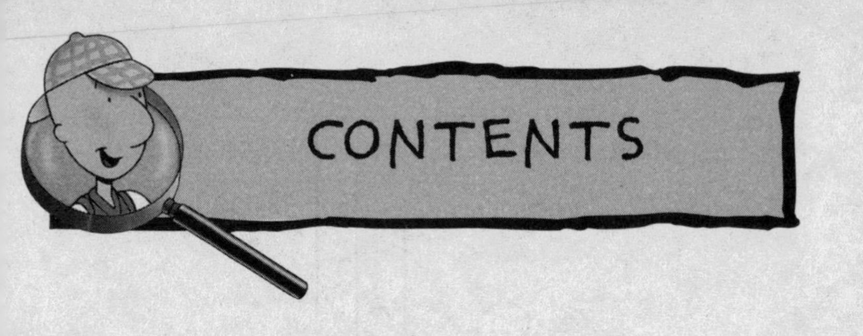

CONTENTS

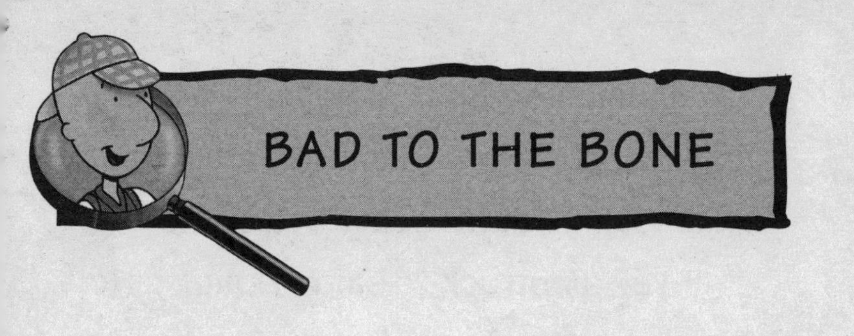

BAD TO THE BONE

Doug was watching some Man O' Steel Man reruns when the doorbell rang. It was Fentruck, carrying a cage covered with a blanket.

"Here they are!" Fentruck said, uncovering the cage. "This is Doblik. And the girl who is chubby is Malinka. Purebred longhaired Yakestonian gerbils. Are they not cute, Doog?"

"Yeah, cute." Doug grinned weakly.

"Oh, Doog, thank you for keeping them. I will be gone only a few days. In this box is everything you need: food, vitamins,

Yakestonian bedtime storybook, and little tiny gerbil blankets." Fentruck fought back tears looking at his pets. "Bye-bye."

"Bye, Fentruck," said Doug. "Hey, where are you going?"

"Oh, Doog, it is most thrilling! My cousin, Grubnik, becomes a citizen tomorrow! I go to attend the ceremony. And after, a delicious feast of Yakestonian delicacies. I will bring to you some treats."

"That's okay, Fentruck," Doug replied, being polite but not wanting to eat Yakestonian pickled trout snout again.

"I must!" Fentruck said. "You have been kind to me. In my country the good neighbor must be rewarded."

"Well . . . okay," Doug said. "Thank you, Fentruck."

* * *

The rest of the day was hard for Doug. It was especially hard keeping the gerbils in their cage.

"He told you to *watch* them, Dougie," Judy sniped. She was in her room, in no mood for interruptions.

"I'm watching them, Judy!" Doug said. "I opened the cage for just a second and Malinka shot right out!"

"So don't open it, Einstein."

"Oh, great idea!" Doug said. "I guess I'll just pour the water through the bars and hope they catch it on their little tongues!"

"Not my problem," said Judy. "You'll have an even bigger problem if that rodent gets in my room."

"Please, Judy," Doug said, "I need your

help. Their fur gives me hives and I sneeze when I pick them up."

"Oh, all right," Judy said. "If you find Malinka I'll pick her up, but I'm not looking for her. I'm busy."

"Thanks, Judy," Doug said. "Man, this gerbil-sitting is a lot tougher than I thought."

The doorbell rang. Doug was surprised to find his neighbor there. "Hey, Mr. Dink."

"Hello, Douglas. I was trying out my super-electro-magnified binoculars. . . ."

"Oh, I read about them!" Doug said. "They have a huge range of vision."

"Yes, yes," Mr. Dink said. "Very expensive. Anyway, I was wearing them and I spotted *this*." Mr. Dink held out Malinka. "Your mother said you've been looking for her."

Doug immediately started sneezing,

"Just—achooo—Mr. Dink—achoooooo!" Doug ran back inside. He returned with the cage and held it out. "Put her right in—in—achooooooo!—inside."

Mr. Dink put Malinka in her cage and closed the door.

"Thank-ah-thank-ah—choooooo!" Doug sneezed.

"You're welcome, my boy." Mr. Dink waved. "Such a grateful lad. Brings a tear to my eye."

"Mom," Doug moaned, "have you seen Malinka?" His second day of gerbil-sitting had started off badly.

"Oh, dear, have you lost her again?"

"I can't help it," Doug admitted. "If I get too close, I sneeze and itch. If I stay away,

she jiggles open the door and escapes."

"I'm sorry, dear," said Theda. "But you'll just have to do your best until tonight."

The phone rang and Doug raced to answer it. It was Skeeter. "Hey, Doug, want to go to Swirly's?"

"Sorry, Skeeter," Doug said. "I can't. Malinka is lost again. I've looked for her all morning." As he talked, he looked under the couch. "Hey, there she is! No, that's just Judy's coonskin cap from her anti-gun play, *Annie Get Rid of Your Gun*."

At that moment, Porkchop entered. He began to bark and tug on Doug's pants.

"Hang on, Skeet," Doug said. "Porkchop, cut it out! I'm on the phone!"

Porkchop continued to jump and bark.

"Porkchop, I mean it. This is important!"

Doug said. He returned to the phone. "So anyway, I'm really getting sick of those hairy little rats! I'd like to put them both in a box and ship them back to Yakestonia!"

Shocked, Porkchop gasped and looked at his best friend. Then he quickly disappeared.

"Hey, Skeet, would you help me find her?" Doug asked. "Great! See ya."

"Skeeter's coming over to look for Malinka," Doug said, turning to where Porkchop had been. "Porkchop? Now, where did *he* go?"

When Skeeter arrived, they looked everywhere for the little gerbil. Remembering that Mr. Dink had found her outside, they went out.

"You know, Skeet," Doug complained as they searched near Porkchop's tepee, "I don't like gerbils. They make me a-a-a-*choo*!—sneeze. I didn't know that until I started taking care of them."

From his tepee, Porkchop growled angrily.

"What's the matter, Porkchop?" asked Doug. "Are you mad?"

Porkchop growled louder.

"Well, I'm sorry I was grouchy," Doug said. "Malinka ruined my whole weekend and ah-ah-*achooo!* . . ."

Porkchop barked loudly.

"Okay! Okay!" Doug said. "Skeeter, let's look inside again. Porkchop, please let me know if you see her."

* * *

"Doug, we've looked everywhere," Skeeter said. "You have to tell Fentruck that she's lost."

"I can't!" Doug said.

The doorbell rang. It was Mr. Dink, with Malinka again.

"You found her!" exclaimed Doug. "I'll go get her cage. Hold her, Skeet! Thanks, Mr. Dink!"

"No problem!" Mr. Dink shouted as Doug disappeared. "She was coming out of Porkchop's tepee," he told Skeeter.

"So that's where she was," said Skeeter.

After Doug brought the cage, Skeeter put Malinka inside. As they snapped the cage door shut, the doorbell rang again. It was Fentruck.

"Hello, Doog!" Fentruck smiled. "How

are my little *moushkas*? I hope they were no trouble."

"Are you kidding?" Skeeter said.

"No trouble at all," Doug said quickly. "Here's all their stuff."

"Oh, thank you, Doog. I bring to you the greatest of Yakestonian treats—pickled trout snout. Enjoy!" Fentruck said.

"Oh. Great, Fentruck. Thanks," Doug said weakly. "Good-bye."

"Man, that was close," Doug and Skeeter sighed in unison, closing the door.

The next day, Doug noticed that things weren't quite right. Judy's coonskin cap was missing and she was blaming Doug, since he had seen it last.

Maybe Porkchop saw it, thought Doug heading out to Porkchop's tepee. "Porkchop, have you seen . . . ?"

Inside his tepee, Porkchop growled ferociously when he heard Doug's voice.

"Okay, I get the hint. Are you ever going to forgive me?" Doug sighed, walking back to the house. "This isn't like Porkchop."

"Hey, Doug," honked Skeeter, "what's wrong?"

"Hey, Skeet," Doug said. "Porkchop's been acting weird for two days. I can't figure it out."

"Maybe he's sick, man," said Skeeter.

"Yeah," Doug said. "I'd better take a look at him."

Doug sneaked toward Porkchop's tepee. As he got closer, he sneezed. Porkchop growled and Doug backed away.

"Man," Skeeter said, "Porkchop is acting just like a bad dog. Are you getting a cold, man?"

"Douglas," Theda called.

"We're out here, Mom," replied Doug.

"There's some milk and beet-chip

cookies in the kitchen. Help yourselves," said Theda.

"Thanks," Doug said, heading into the kitchen.

As Doug poured a big glass of milk, Porkchop entered with his Big Swig mug.

"Hey, Porkchop, you want some water?" Doug asked.

Porkchop shook his head "no" and held the mug out toward the milk.

"More milk?" Doug asked. "Man, you're drinking lots of milk lately!"

Porkchop growled.

"All right, all right! Milk it is," Doug said. He handed Porkchop the mug. Then he began to sneeze.

"Man," Skeeter said, "that's some cold you've got. It comes and goes so quickly."

"Skeeter, this is weird," Doug sniffed. "I've never sneezed like this except around Fentruck's gerbils. You don't think they've come back?"

"Go call Fentruck," said Skeeter.

"Good idea, Skeet," Doug said.

Fentruck answered right away. "No, Doog, now I am looking at Doblik and Malinka. But they seem unhappy since I bring them home. Maybe they like to live with you," he said sadly.

"No," Doug said quickly. "In fact, Malinka kept trying to escape. I don't think she liked my house at all."

"Maybe. Well, good-bye, Doog," said Fentruck.

Doug turned to Skeeter. "He said the gerbils are sad, Skeeter. What would

make gerbils sad? And why am I still sneezing? I've got to solve this problem so I can focus on what's wrong with Porkchop. What's he doing with all that milk? And where's Judy's coonskin cap?"

As Doug thought aloud, he scratched a hive on his hand. He remembered touching Porkchop's paw when he gave the dog the milk. "Hmmm," he said, "I wonder . . ." Suddenly, he knew what to do!

"Skeeter," Doug said, "I think Porkchop has the answers. Can you distract him while I go inside his tepee?"

"Let's go!" said Skeeter.

Is Porkchop really bad to the bone? Will Doug ever stop sneezing? And who will eat the Yakestonian pickled trout snout?

Skeeter sat where Porkchop could see him eat a huge slice of bone pizza. Porkchop had been in his tepee all day, except for quick trips to get milk. He was hungry.

"Mmmmmm! That's good eatin'!" slurped Skeeter. "Hey, Porkchop! Want some?"

While Porkchop took the bait, Doug tiptoed to the tepee and peeked inside. He immediately sneezed.

Porkchop realized he'd been tricked. He slapped his forehead with one paw, then ran inside to hover protectively over Judy's coonskin cap. It was filled with a litter of tiny Yakestonian gerbil babies! Porkchop howled sadly, pleading at Doug with his eyes.

"Achoooo!" Doug moved back from

the door to catch his breath. "Oh, I get it, Porkchop," he said, "I said some terrible things about gerbils. I'm sorry. No wonder you were afraid to let me know about the babies. I was just upset, Porkchop. I'm sorry. I love these little animals!"

"Hey, Doug," said Skeeter looking in the tepee, "that coonskin cap looks a little like Malinka."

“Let’s call Fentruck so these babies can see their parents!” said Doug. Porkchop barked happily.

PATTI'S POLITICAL PERIL

"I am so mad!" Patti said, throwing another poster away. "These posters are awful!"

"I know," Doug said. Patti was running for Seventh-Grade Student Government Representative against Beebe Bluff and Chalky Studebaker. Doug, Patti's campaign manager, had helped her make posters. The posters had a photo of Patti and said VOTE FOR PATTI—SHE'S GOT SOMETHING SPECIAL! However, someone had put red dots all over her picture, giving the phrase *She's Got Something Special* a whole new meaning.

"Who would do such a thing?" Patti asked.

"Maybe one of your opponents?" Doug said.

"Beebe and Chalky wouldn't," Patti said. "They're my friends."

I know Patti's right, Doug thought. But if it's not Beebe or Chalky, who could it be?

The next day, Doug and Patti came to school with new posters.

As they passed Patti's locker, Doug said, "Patti, why don't you practice your speech for this afternoon? I'll take care of these."

"Thanks, Doug." Patti smiled as she turned to her locker. There was a flyer jammed in the door.

"Oh, no! Not again!"

"What is it, Patti?" Doug asked.

"Look at this!" She handed him the flyer. It read,

CHALKY STUDEBAKER DROPS OUT OF RACE

CLAIMS PATTI MAYONNAISE IS GREEDY!

It featured a photograph of Patti taking money from a baby in a carriage.

"I wasn't stealing!" Patti said. "A baby was eating play money! I gave it to his mother so he wouldn't get hurt!"

"Who would do that, Patti? Do you think Chalky . . ."

"Doug," Patti said, "you can't accuse people with no proof. Chalky wouldn't do that."

"Let's find out," Doug said, seeing Chalky coming down the hall reading the flyer. "Hey, Chalky," Doug said, "I see you got a flyer, too. What's going on?"

"Hey, Doug," Chalky said. "I'm glad I ran

CHALKY STUDEBAKER
DROPS OUT OF RACE
CLAIMS PATTI MAYONNAISE
IS GREEDY!

into you two. I guess it's no secret anymore. I told Mr. Bone after school yesterday that I was dropping out. I'm just too busy. But I never said you were greedy, Patti."

"I know," said Patti. "So who could have done this?"

"I have no idea," said Chalky. "Except . . . there *was* someone in the office when I went to talk to Mr. Bone. A new kid, I think. Maybe he heard us talking."

"But if he's new, why would he care who wins?" asked Patti.

"I don't know," said Chalky. "Anyway, you've got my vote, Patti."

"Thanks, Chalky." Patti turned to Doug. "Now, what do we do?"

"Look at this!" exclaimed Doug, holding

the flyer. "These are printed on gilt-edged rice paper! Who else but Beebe could afford that?"

"She wouldn't, Doug," Patti said.

"Okay, okay," Doug said. "Come on. We can't let this get us down."

Later that afternoon, Beebe stopped Patti at her locker. "Patti, your speech was great!"

"Thanks Beebe. Your idea to fill every Girls' Room with potpourri is wonderful! But I don't think I stand a chance after these awful smear tactics."

"Don't worry," Beebe said. "Everyone knows those things aren't true. I hope you know that I had nothing to do with those flyers. My Beautiful Bathrooms Initiative is

a cause worth fighting for, but I'd never let it hurt our friendship."

"I know, Beebe," Patti smiled. "Well, see ya!" She sighed as she walked away. She had never really thought Beebe was involved. Still, it was nice to hear her say so.

Just then, Patti saw Doug and Skeeter standing in the hall with a crowd of students.

"Hey, guys," Patti said. "What's everybody looking at?"

"You don't want to know," Doug said with a sigh.

"What now?" she asked, pushing past Doug.

A huge poster hung on the wall. It read, PATTI MAYONNAISE—ANIMAL ABUSER. There were three pictures on it. The first was of

PATTI MAYONNAISE
ANIMAL ABUSER

a frightened puppy. The second showed the puppy being dragged by a leash. In the third, Patti wore a fur jacket that had the same spots as the puppy's coat!

"I can't believe this!" cried Patti. "I'd never wear a dog-fur coat. Yuck!"

"Besides," said Skeeter, "it would smell really bad in the rain."

"You know, Skeeter," Doug said, "not many kids can afford to print up expensive

posters and flyers like these. You're Beebe's campaign manager; you don't think she's . . ."

"Beebe wouldn't do that to Patti, Doug," Skeeter said. "Besides, she could never keep a secret this long. Hey Patti, does that coat have any fleas?"

"Skeeter!" Patti shouted, "I didn't make a coat out of that puppy! He needed a home so I took him to the animal shelter!"

"Oh," said Skeeter. "Sorry."

The next morning, as Ms. Kristal turned on the television, she said, "Take your seats. It's time for the *News for Kids Weekly Update*."

The *Weekly Update* began as usual. Suddenly a voice cut in. "We interrupt this

program for a special report. Aliens invade politics at Beebe Bluff Middle School! Patti Mayonnaise—friendly, All-Tri-County girl and candidate for Seventh-Grade Representative—is really an alien from the planet Cryptosporidium! She is extremely dangerous. Don't let her melt your brain, and above all, do *not* vote for her in today's election. Stop the aliens while you still can! Thank you. This announcement was paid for by CRAB, Citizens to Repel Aliens from Bluffington."

Patti's jaw dropped. Her classmates giggled and whispered.

After class, Doug stopped Patti and said, "Come on! I've got an idea."

They raced down the hall as Doug said, "Who do we know at school with access

to video equipment and computers who could print up flyers like these?"

"The A.V. nerds!" Patti shouted.

They burst into the A.V. room. Doug said, "All right, somebody here owes Patti an explanation. Come clean now before things get ugly."

"He did it!" Elmo, Lincoln, and Brian shouted, all pointing at Larry.

"Larry?" Patti said, "Why?"

"I had to," Larry sobbed. "He said if I didn't I'd never see my pet rat again."

"He kidnapped your rat?" gasped Doug.

"No," said Larry. "But I thought he might."

"Who?" said Doug.

"The new kid," Larry answered. "He wears dark glasses and has black hair. I'm sorry, Patti."

"That's okay, Larry," said Patti as they left.

"Let's see if anybody knows this new kid," Doug said.

"You and Skeeter talk to the boys," said Patti. "Beebe and I will question the girls. See ya!"

The grapevine at Beebe Bluff Middle School worked quickly. By the time the bell rang ending their next class, the young detectives knew that the new kid was in shop class. They raced through the hallway to catch him.

"He's over there!" shouted Skeeter.

Patti, Skeeter, and Beebe watched helplessly as the stranger ducked out a side door, but Doug got to a window in time to see him jump into a black car and drive away.

"Kids aren't supposed to drive!" Skeeter said, joining Doug at the window. "Now he's *really* in trouble."

"If he's really a *kid*," said Patti. "He's very tall. Doug, did you get his license number?"

"Yes. BLF-CO3," Doug replied. "I'll go see Mr. Dink after school. He'll help me find out who it is."

"You know," Beebe mused, "there's something familiar about that car. . . ."

Mr. Dink loved to help Doug. "Why, sure, Douglas, my boy," he chuckled. "I've got just the thing. The Krime-Katcher Fact Kruncher 2001. Just type in your clues and the Kruncher does the rest. Now, what's that license number?"

Lights flashed, bells clanged, whistles blew. Out popped a tiny piece of paper. "Here's your answer, Douglas," Mr. Dink said.

"The car belongs to . . ." Doug stopped suddenly. "Of course. Mr. Dink, may I use your phone? I've got to tell Patti to meet me at Beebe's."

When Doug and Patti rang the bell, Skeeter and Beebe were already there.

"What's up?" said Beebe.

Who is the mysterious new kid? Does he really have a driver's license? And where did Patti get that fake dog-fur coat?

"I think I know who's smearing Patti," said Doug. "All the clues point to someone who wants Patti to lose the election. Now, we know the new kid used Larry to print the material. He looks old for seventh grade, and I just found out that the license plate belongs to a BLUFFCO car."

"I knew I'd seen that car," said Beebe. "It's one of Daddy's. Why was it at school?"

Doug answered, "Because your Dad has been running around this school disguised as a student to help you win."

"Daddy!" Beebe screamed.

Dear Journal,

Well, all's well that ends well. Patti won the election. Mr. Bluff apologized to Beebe and Patti for interfering, and he threw a victory celebration for Patti at Funkytown to make it up to her. He also announced at school that all those posters were lies. Of course, everyone knew that already. I guess real friends always believe the best about you no matter what.

THE THIEF IN THE FUNNIE HOUSE

"Okay, where is it?" Phil Funnie said looking at the coffee table.

"Where is what, dear?" Theda called from the kitchen.

"It was right here when I left for work this morning. I just don't understand . . ." Phil muttered, looking under the sofa.

"I can't hear you, dear," replied Theda.

"My Psychedelic Fuzz peace chain from our last performance at Twigstock. It was here this morning and now it's gone," moaned Phil.

"Oh, that," Theda said. "I'm sure it's here somewhere."

"I hope so," Phil said, looking worried. "I promised a customer I'd bring it to the store. He was a big fan and wants his picture taken with it."

"How can anyone get so excited over an old necklace?" Theda wondered.

"It's a peace chain, Theda," Phil said. "You know, there are still some people out there who enjoyed our music."

"I love your music, honey!" said Theda. "But that necklace . . ."

"Peace chain!" Phil corrected.

"Yes, dear, peace chain. It's just that it's furry, pink-and-green-and-purple, and it doesn't match anything in this room, sweetie," Theda complained.

"You think it's ugly? Dearest, you've never liked that chain, have you?" asked Phil.

"Well . . ." Theda paused. "Maybe it would look better in your darkroom, darling."

"Isn't it funny that suddenly it's disappeared, honey lumpkin?" Phil said suspiciously. "Maybe it's sitting in a garbage truck right now."

"Philip Funnie, are you accusing me of throwing your necklace away?"

"PEACE CHAIN!" insisted Phil.

"Well, if that's how you feel, sugar pie, you can cook your own dinner tonight!" Theda stomped out.

"That's just fine, because we're going out to dinner, remember, lovey?" Phil called after her.

"Fine. Then after dinner I'm not speaking to you, pumpkin!" Theda yelled back.

"Doug! Judy! Come here, please," Phil called.

"Hey, Dad. What's all the racket?" Doug

asked as he and Judy joined Phil.

"Your mother and I had a little disagreement. I can't seem to find my peace chain and . . ."

"You mean that ridiculous necklace?" asked Judy.

"Peace ch—oh, never mind," Phil said. "Anyway, I got a little upset. Now, I have to apologize to your mother. Then we're going to the Dinks' for dinner. You can order pizza from Speedy Pizza. Keep an eye on Cleopatra Dirtbike. She's been getting into everything lately."

"Sure, Dad," said Judy. "We'll take care of everything."

"Thanks. I knew I could count on you." Phil left the room.

"Great!" Doug grinned. "Pizza and the

whole house to ourselves. What could be better than that? I'll order the pizza."

"Order one with extra anchovies," Judy said. "I'm going to the kitchen to make some tea, so watch Cleopatra."

"Sure," Doug mumbled absentmindedly as he dialed the phone and read the pizza menu.

Phil and Theda entered the living room laughing. Their little spat had ended. Theda walked to the table by the sofa.

"Just a second, dear," Theda said, reaching into the sofa cushions. "Oh, dear!"

"What's wrong?" Phil asked.

"Has anyone seen my brooch? It was on that end table this afternoon," said Theda.

"Which brooch?" Phil asked.

"My grandmother's," replied Theda, still searching.

"Oh," said Phil. "It'll turn up. You look fine without it. Hurry. We'll be late."

"You never liked that brooch, did you?" said Theda.

"Well-l-l-l-l . . ."

"I'll have you know, Phil Funnie, that unlike your ugly old necklace . . ."

"Peace chain!" interrupted Phil.

"Whatever," Theda said. "My brooch is a valuable heirloom."

"Whoever thought of designing a pin in the shape of a pancreas?" Phil said. "Old or not, it's a pancreas."

"The pancreas is vital!" Theda said. "Mankind would suffer greatly without the

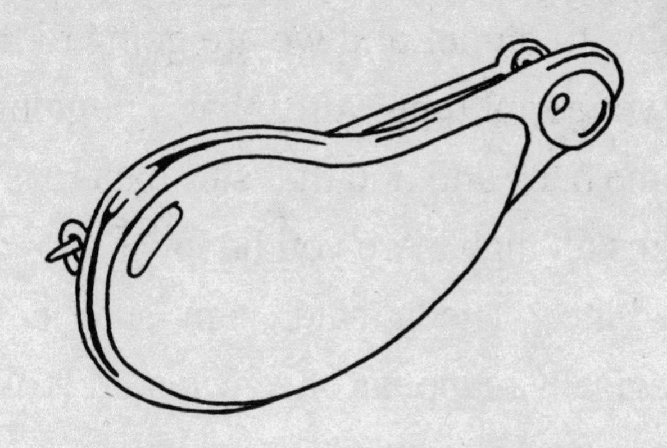

pancreas. Would you rather it be something common, like a heart? *Everybody* wears heart-shaped jewelry. My pancreas is extraordinary and I wear it proudly! By the way, dearest, it's odd that it's gone so suddenly."

"Sweetness, are you suggesting . . . ?" Phil paused.

"If the *necklace* fits, honey, wear it," Theda said accusingly.

"Okay, darling," Phil said. "We are

going to dinner and we are going to have a wonderful time. After that, I'm going to come back and find that silly pancreas if it takes all night. Are you happy?"

"Fine," Theda said. "I'm sure it will magically reappear once *you* start looking for it, lambie pie."

Phil Funnie sighed, "Good night, son."

"What was that all about?" Judy asked, entering the room with Dirtbike in her arms.

"Mom lost her favorite brooch and thinks Dad hid it," said Doug.

"The pancreas?" Judy asked. "I hope he doesn't find it. As the oldest female in the family, guess who's next in line to wear it? Yick!"

Judy put Dirtbike on the floor. "By the way, Dougie, you let Cleopatra get away. I

found her in the kitchen by the trash can. She's so cute! When I threw out my tea bag, she said, 'All gone.'"

"Oh, sorry," Doug said. "I got distracted. I'm not used to Mom and Dad arguing. Hey, maybe I can find their stuff."

"Suit yourself. I wouldn't worry," said Judy.

At that moment, Porkchop came into the room, folded his arms, and began tapping his foot impatiently.

"Hey, Porkchop. What's the matter?" Doug said.

Porkchop placed an invitation in his hand.

"Oh, yeah," Doug read, "The French Poetry Festival is tonight. You'd better hurry or you'll be late."

Porkchop shook his head stubbornly.

Doug was confused. "You're not going? Why not? You even bought a new beret for the occasion."

Porkchop made a "Right!" face and continued tapping his foot impatiently.

"I don't get it, Porkchop," Doug said. "Where's your beret? Can't you find it? Where did you see it last?" Doug asked.

Porkchop pointed to the sofa where Judy sat, sipping a mug of Tranquillity Tea.

"It has to be here somewhere," Doug said. "Have you looked . . ." Porkchop stopped him, shaking his head yes.

"Where could it be?" Doug thought aloud.

Porkchop growled and looked at Judy.

"No, you don't think . . . ?"

Porkchop interrupted him again, nodding his head. He growled at Judy.

"Dougie," Judy sighed, "what's wrong with that dog of yours?"

"Judy," Doug said carefully, "have you seen Porkchop's new beret?"

"No. Now make him stop growling," she replied.

"Porkchop thought you might have it," Doug continued.

"Well, I don't," Judy said. "Go away."

Porkchop growled softly.

"But, Judy . . ." Doug said.

"Listen, you two, I haven't seen it. My beret is great; I don't need another," she said.

There was a knock at the door. "There's the pizza," said Judy. "If you want to live

long enough to eat it, you and your dog had better leave me alone." Judy went to answer the door.

"Sorry, Porkchop," Doug said. "Can't you go without it? We'll find it later."

Porkchop stomped past Judy and the deliveryman, growling as he left the house.

Judy returned with the pizza. "Honestly, Dougie, that dog . . . where's Cleopatra?"

They ran searching for the missing Funnie.

"I found her," Doug called from the kitchen. "She was throwing away her rattle, but I got there before she knocked the trash can over. She's not going anywhere now," he said, putting her in her playpen.

"Hey, where's my mug?" Judy said suddenly.

"What mug?" Doug said.

"My Shakespeare-on-Ice mug. It was right here on the coffee table with Tranquillity Tea in it." She thought a moment. "That dog! Porkchop must have

taken it because he thought I took his hat! That little fleabag!"

"Porkchop wouldn't do that. He walked right past you. He didn't have it," said Doug. "Besides, Porkchop doesn't have fleas."

"Then he hid it," Judy said. "You're probably in on it, too. When you decide to return my mug, I'll be in my room. And, Dougie, Cleopatra's your responsibility!"

"Fine!" Doug shouted. He turned to his baby sister. "What a night, Dirtbike. Where could all that stuff be?"

Dirtbike giggled and threw her rattle. "Aawl gone," she said.

The next morning things were unusually tense. Phil and Theda muttered at each other, and Judy and Porkchop

growled at each other. The only happy person in the house was Dirtbike and she couldn't talk much. After breakfast, Doug had had enough.

There has got to be an explanation, Doug thought, *and I'm going to find it.*

In his room, Doug made out a list of clues. First, his dad lost his peace chain, which was on the coffee table. Second, his mom's brooch disappeared from the sofa's end table. Then Porkchop lost his beret from the sofa and Judy's mug vanished from the coffee table. Everything had disappeared from the living room! But who could have taken them? There was not one person who could have committed all four thefts. Or was there? Suddenly, Doug thought he knew the answer!

Will Phil Funnie's furry necklace—peace chain, that is—be found? Will Judy pulverize Porkchop? What will disappear next? And what does a pancreas look like, anyway?

Doug raced downstairs. Everyone was arguing except Dirtbike. As he watched, Doug saw her pick up the remote control and crawl toward the kitchen.

"Hey! Look!" Doug pointed at Dirtbike.

Everyone followed her as she stood up, threw the remote control into the trash can, and giggled, "Aawl gone." The culprit was found!

The Funnies retrieved their missing treasures from the trash can—and a few items they hadn't known were missing. They all laughed and apologized to each other.

Suddenly, Judy asked, "Where's Cleopatra?"

"Where's the remote control?" asked Phil.

They heard a flushing sound, followed by "Aawl gone."

"Dirtbike!" they all cried, running to the bathroom.

It had been a great day at Beebe Bluff Middle School. Doug had aced his science test, Patti Mayonnaise had sat next to him during the pep rally, and Mr. Bone had spent most of the morning at the dentist, which made all the students happy.

"Gee, Skeet," Doug joked, "wouldn't it be great if Mr. Bone came in only half a day every day?"

"Yeah," Skeeter replied. "Maybe he needs braces, too."

"Yeah, that might keep him at the

dentist a lot." Doug laughed. "I have to stop by the science lab. Wanna come?"

"Sure," Skeeter replied.

As they walked to the lab they spotted Mr. Bone walking toward them. He suddenly clapped his hands to the sides of his head, his eyes darting around as if he were looking for something. Then, he backed against the wall, nervously nodding his head.

"What's he doing?" Doug asked Skeeter.

"Beats me," said Skeeter. "Mr. Bone is weird, but this is weird even for him."

As they got close to Mr. Bone, Doug said, "Hey, Mr. Bone. Is everything okay?"

"Of course everything is okay!" Mr. Bone snapped. "Why do you ask? I never

said anything wasn't okay!" Then he stomped down the hall.

"Gee," Skeeter said. "I guess everything's okay."

"Are you kidding?" Doug said. "That was over the edge."

Skeeter said, "Did you notice that sound? When we got close to him I heard something but I couldn't figure out what."

"Now that you mention it, yeah," Doug said, "I could barely hear it. It sounded familiar, a little like yodeling."

"Well," Skeeter honked, "I have to go help my dad in the yard today. Mom says we need some father-son time."

Doug couldn't stop thinking about Mr. Bone. His strange behavior was still bothering Doug the next day at school. He and

Skeeter saw Mr. Bone in the hall again after science lab. Suddenly, he went into the strange dance again. He backed into the wall, nodding his head.

"Come on, Skeeter," Doug whispered. "We've got to figure this out."

They walked up to Mr. Bone and said, "Hey, Mr. Bone."

Mr. Bone jumped. "Why are you two spying on me?" he asked. "Didn't I tell you everything was okay? Perfectly okay. Okay?"

"We thought you were looking for something," Doug said. "Can we help you?"

"It just so happens that I felt a drop of water on my head and I thought there was a leak in the roof. If anybody asks, that's what I'll tell them. Got it?"

"Got it," the boys answered as they left.

"Skeeter," Doug said. "Something very weird *is* going on."

"I've got it! I know what it is!" Skeeter said.

"What?" Doug asked.

"That yodeling sound," said Skeeter. "I heard it again when we got near Mr. Bone. Remember that science-fiction movie we saw, *It Came from Somewhere Else*?"

"Yeah," Doug said.

"It sounded just like the music they played when the aliens took over someone's brain!" Skeeter said.

"You're right," said Doug with a gasp.

"Are you thinking what I'm thinking?" Skeeter asked.

"Mr. Bone is being brainwashed by an alien!" they cried.

"Who can we ask about weird alien behavior?" said Doug.

Instantly, they both knew exactly who to ask. "Al and Moo Sleech!"

Al and Moo were interested in Doug and Skeeter's story. They "ooohed," "aaahed," and giggled with excitement.

"We have been waiting for this to happen, Doug Funnie," Moo giggled.

"Yes, Doug Funnie," said Al. "Who would have thought that Mr. Bone would be the Chosen One. I am alien green with envy."

"But guys," Doug interrupted. "We can't let aliens take over Mr. Bone's brain!"

"Once chosen, nothing can be done," Al said.

"Unless the aliens agree to switch specimens. If so, tell them to choose me," said Moo.

"No, me," said Al.

"No, me. I said it first," argued Moo.

"Okay! We'll send them for both of you," said Doug.

"Joy! Rapture! Six-point-seven! Six-point-seven-seven!" sang the brothers.

"Thanks, guys," Doug sighed as they walked away.

"They were no help," Doug said. "Who can we talk to that won't think we're nuts?"

"How about Fentruck?" said Skeeter. "He lives with Mr. Bone. I bet he's noticed something."

"Great idea, Skeeter," Doug said. "This is a good time to talk. Mr. Bone's gone to his yodeling club meeting."

"Oh, Doog," Fentruck said with a sigh. "I am glad you ask me these things. I see

him do the strange dance at home also, but there is more."

"More?" Doug asked. "Like what?"

"He is always softly yodeling a song sounding like the Yakestonian National Anthem. Also, you know the Young Yakestonian Yodelers arrive soon for their Tri-County tour?" Fentruck continued.

"Yeah, I heard that on the radio," Doug answered.

"Mr. Bone was very excited for the arrival of the Yak Yodelers. Before he went to the dentist, he was concerned about the landing of their aircraft and the heli-port's construction. Now, he does not speak of it," Fentruck said.

"Really," said Skeeter.

"Oh, yes," nodded Fentruck. "He walks

the field behind our house at night for hours, looking at the sky. What must we do, Doog?"

Doug thought for a moment and then said, "Let's spend the night with Fentruck. If Mr. Bone takes a walk, we'll follow him and see what's happening."

"Oh, thank you so lot, Doog," said Fentruck. "It is good to have a friend like you."

That night, the boys watched from Fentruck's window. Mr. Bone finally appeared. He walked through the field looking up at the sky. The boys followed him. Just as they got close enough for a good look, Skeeter stepped in a rabbit hole, tripped over a dead tree branch, and landed right on top of Mr. Bone.

"Hey, Mr. Bone," Skeeter honked.

"Okay, Mr. Trip-on-Me-in-the-Dark, this must stop! I will not be spied on!" shouted Mr. Bone.

"Please, do not be angry with them," Fentruck said. "I asked for their help. I worry

about the oddness of your behaviors."

"Well," Mr. Bone said. "If it's any of your business, Mr. Nosey-Pants, I have been hearing strange noises lately. Voices yodeling the Yakestonian National Anthem or that theme from *It Came from Somewhere Else*. I hear it only when I'm near the science lab or out in this field. The signals are stronger than ever tonight. Maybe someone, somewhere wants to contact me. I think they've chosen me because I speak a universal language."

"A universal language?" Doug asked.

"Yodeling," said Mr. Bone. "The voices are so strong because this must be our appointed meeting place."

Just then Doug noticed a large radio

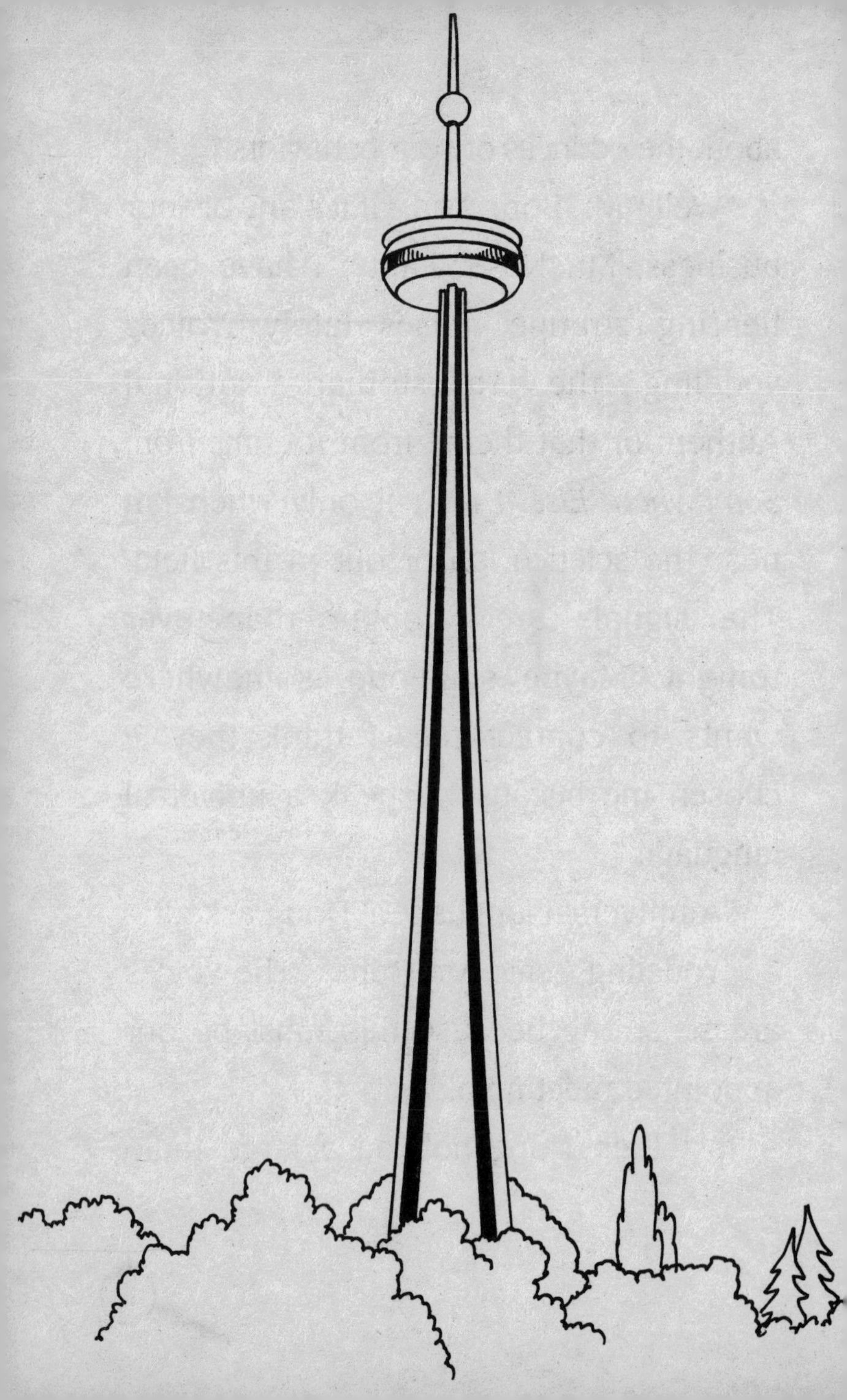

tower at the edge of the field. He thought for a minute.

"Mr. Bone, where did the school install that new power antenna?" Doug asked.

"Right over the science lab," said Mr. Bone.

"By any chance, did these noises begin right after you got your tooth filled?" Doug continued.

"Yes, that's right." Mr. Bone nodded.

"And you've been hearing that strange yodeling," Doug thought aloud. "Hmmm."

Is Mr. Bone being brainwashed by aliens? Will yodeling become our universal language? Or is the science lab the control center for an international yodeling conspiracy?

"Mr. Bone, I think I know what's been . . ." Doug started, but he was interrupted by the loud whirring of an approaching aircraft.

"They're here, they're here!" Mr. Bone shouted. "The aliens are here! Quick, cover your brains!"

"They are here!" Fentruck shouted and clapped his hands. "Oh, Mr. Bone, how did you know they would land here? You are a genius!"

As the flying craft landed, Skeeter said, "Wow, I didn't know aliens traveled in helicopters."

Before Fentruck could answer, human-like beings wearing lederhosen stepped off the craft and began walking toward them. Mr. Bone fainted. Fentruck screamed, "You are here!" and ran toward them.

Doug said, "They aren't aliens, Skeet. They are the Young Yakestonian Yodelers. They landed here because the heliport is being repaired."

"Oh yes, that's right," said Mr. Bone, waking up. "I forgot. I haven't been able to think of anything except these awful voices in my head! You've got to help me, boys!"

"That's what I was trying to explain," Doug said. "Your new filling picked up radio signals from the radio station. They've been broadcasting ads and playing the Yodelers singing the Yakestonian National Anthem—which sounds like the theme from *It Came from Somewhere Else*. The antennae here and at school made the signals come in clearly."

As Doug, Skeeter, and Mr. Bone spoke, they were joined by Fentruck and the Yak Yodelers. Mr. Bone, ignoring the fact that seconds before, he had believed them to be aliens, said, "Welcome, Yodeling Yaks! Would you all come in for some cookies and yak milk?"

"Why, yes," their leader said. "That would be better than a hog's snout!"

"Well, come along!" Mr. Bone said. "I'll get you all fixed up . . . right after I call my dentist!"

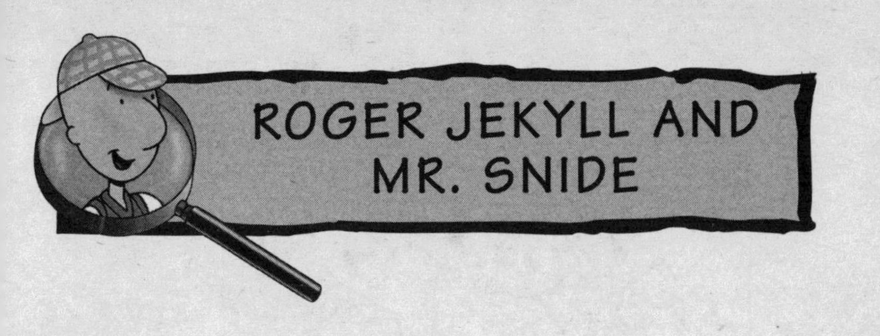

ROGER JEKYLL AND MR. SNIDE

"Man, what a hot day," Doug said. "It's so hot that my paints are melting."

"What is that?" Beebe said, looking over Doug's shoulder.

"It's my masterpiece," Doug smiled proudly. "How do you like it?"

"You're kidding, right?" Beebe said as she burst into laughter. "Patti, Chalky, Skeeter! Look at this!"

Soon everyone stood around Doug's entry in the Bluffington Art Contest. They laughed so hard they fell down.

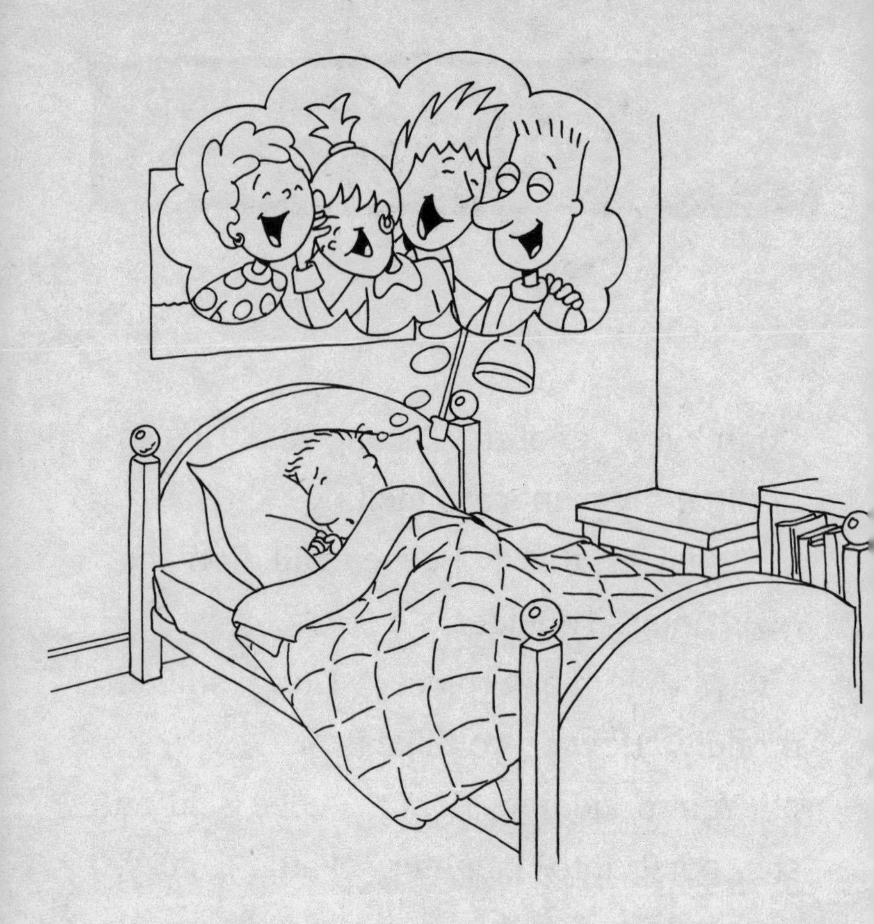

"Stop it!" cried Doug. "Stop laughing! It's good, I tell you, it's good! Stop laaugh-hiiiing!"

Doug sat up straight in his bed. Oh, it

was just a dream, he thought. Wow, it's three o'clock in the morning! Man, I must be so worried about the art contest I'm even dreaming about it. Maybe if I get up and work on it I'll get tired enough to go back to sleep.

Doug went to the living room to work on his painting. He found Porkchop eating popcorn and watching an infomercial.

"Can't sleep, Porkchop?" Doug said. "Me, neither. Mind if I join you?"

"Hi, I'm Joe Schmoudini," went the infomercial. "Are you tired, yet can't sleep? Are you stressed? Are your dreams turning into nightmares? Have I got a cure for you! Just order my tape series, *How to Hypnotize Your Friends for Fun and Profit.* These tapes are the ticket to everything

SELF HYP
Joe Schmouldini

you've ever wanted! Got an enemy? Make him cluck like a chicken! Want more money? Hypnotize your boss! He'll give you that raise! Be the life of the party! Have friends, friends, friends, whether they like you or not! It even works on that lazy mutt lying next to you! Make him serve *you* for a change!"

Porkchop growled.

"That's enough of that," Doug said. "Let's go to bed." Porkchop agreed.

The next morning the phone rang as Doug dressed for school.

"Hey, Funnie." It was Roger Klotz. "Could you use a ride to school this morning?"

Naturally, Doug was suspicious. "Why, Roger?"

"No reason," said Roger. "It popped into

my mind, that's all. So, what do you say, good buddy?"

"Okay, I guess. I'll see you later," Doug said, hanging up the phone. "I must be crazy to trust Roger."

Doug waited on his stoop for twenty minutes with no sign of Roger. "I should have known!" Doug said. "Roger just wanted to make me late. I'd better go."

As Doug headed to school, he heard a car behind him. It was Roger's limousine. Great. *Now* he gets here, thought Doug. Roger's car slowed down and Doug walked up to it. Then Roger popped out of the sunroof holding a bucket of water, which he dumped on Doug just before the car sped away.

Doug was late for school and he was still steaming about having to change clothes when he arrived. Roger! Doug thought. I can't believe he did that! I'm going to give him a piece of my mind—right after class.

Doug sat down. Behind him, Roger

asked quietly, "Doug, would you like my new pen?" He didn't mention the morning's prank. "Oh, by the way," Roger said, "Good luck in the art contest."

Doug was so surprised by Roger's behavior that all he could say was "Thanks."

The bell rang and class was over. Doug turned to let Roger have it, but before he could say a word, Roger saw the pen in Doug's hand and said, "How'd a loser like you get an expensive pen like that, Funnie?"

Doug looked at Roger in shock. "Roger, you just gave it to me."

"Why would I do that? You think I'm the Give-a-Gift Foundation? Give it back!" Roger demanded.

Doug did.

At lunch Doug and his friends discussed Roger's strange behavior.

"I saw him open the door for Connie," said Patti. "And five minutes later, he knocked her books out of her hands."

"He was so polite in P.E. today," Chalky said, "that Coach Spitz actually let him referee tryouts for the new boxing course."

"How did that go?" asked Doug.

"Great!" said Chalky, "until the end of the first round. Then, right between rounds, he punched Skunky Beaumont in the nose. When the bell rang to start the next round, he went back and called the fight as if nothing had happened."

"That's really weird, man," said

Skeeter. "I thought he acted funny today, too. You know how Roger sticks that sign on my back?"

"Kick me?" asked Doug.

"Yeah," said Skeeter. "And then he . . ."

"Kicks you?" said Doug.

"Right. Well, he did it again today between classes, but just as the next class started, I heard him tell his gang not to kick me because it was mean."

"Roger said that?" asked Chalky.

"Yeah," said Skeeter. "Weird, huh?"

Just then, Roger entered the lunch-room, causing all sorts of trouble. He shot mega spitballs at the A.V. nerds' table, made fun of Fentruck's accent, and tried to pull the chair out from under Patti as she sat down. Just as he was about to get

in trouble with Mr. Bone again, the bell rang and lunch ended. Roger excused himself, picked up his tray, took it to the kitchen, and offered to help the kitchen staff with the dishes!

"Doug," said Skeeter, "I think we need to call a doctor. Roger's sick!"

"What do you think is wrong with him?" asked Doug.

"Maybe he's caught some jungle virus," said Skeeter. "Except he hasn't been to the jungle. Maybe it's a jungle *gym* virus."

"No, Skeet," Doug said. "Let's talk to Roger's gang. Maybe they know something."

A few minutes later, the two detectives had found Willy, Ned, and Boomer.

"Hey, guys," said Doug. "Have you noticed anything strange about Roger lately?"

"What's it to you, Funnie?" asked Boomer.

Doug said, "Don't you think he's acting sorta weird?"

"Well," said Ned, "maybe. I mean, one minute he's really, um . . ."

"Nice?" said Doug.

"Yeah, nice," said Ned. "I don't know what to do when he's nice. And then, later, he's really, uh . . ."

"Mean?" said Doug.

"Yeah, mean. That's easier to understand," Ned said.

"Can you describe what happens?" asked Doug.

"Well," Willy spoke up, "in first period, he was, like, normal . . ."

"Mean?" said Doug.

"Yeah, normal." Willy went on, "Right up until class started. Then, he stopped pulling Beebe's hair, walked straight to his desk, and pulled his homework out of his folder."

"Roger did homework?" asked Boomer. He was visibly shaken.

"Yeah," said Willy. "It's kinda scary. What do you think is wrong with him?"

"I don't know," said Doug. "We need more information. Come on, Skeeter. Let's go see Roger."

"I wonder which Roger we're going to meet, Skeeter," said Doug. As they walked

to the Klotz Mansion, they heard the sound of glass breaking, shouting, and Roger laughing.

"I think I know," said Skeeter.

Doug rang the doorbell. The shouting and laughter stopped immediately, and Roger politely answered the door. "Well," he said, "what a pleasant surprise. Mother! Mr. Funnie and Mr. Valentine are here! Do come in." He showed them to the living room. "Sit down, my friends. It is so good of you to come. Can I get you some cookies?"

"Thanks, Roger," Doug said.

While Roger went to the kitchen, Doug and Skeeter discussed the situation. Doug said, "Well, we know that the nice Roger can come out anytime, anywhere. But he always seems to come out right before or right after something starts or ends. I wonder why?"

Skeeter answered, "I don't know, man. Maybe he just wants to scare us."

Roger returned with a tray of cookies and the boys began to eat. Just then, the telephone rang. Snatching Doug's cookie away before he could eat it, Roger grabbed the phone and shouted, "Yeah, what do you want?" Roger had changed again!

Doug looked at Skeeter. "Are you thinking what I'm thinking?" he said.

"I am, if you're thinking, 'let's get out of here!'" said Skeeter.

Roger—the old Roger—slammed down the phone. Then he said, "What are you creeps doing here? Beat it!"

"I don't think so," said Doug. "We're here and we're not going anywhere."

Skeeter moaned, "Oh, no."

"Well, that's too bad, Funnie," said Roger. "'Cause you know what I have to do now."

"What?" asked Doug.

"Cream you!" shouted Roger.

"I don't think you will," said Doug. "In fact, I think you're going to give me another cookie."

"What's wrong with you, Doug?" asked Skeeter, hiding behind the sofa. "Are you trying to get us creamed?"

"No, Skeet," Doug said. "Just solving a mystery. So where's my cookie, Roger?"

Will Roger cream Doug before the mystery is solved? Will Doug get a cookie before Roger becomes nice again? Is there any milk to go with the cookies?

"I'll get you your cookie, Funnie-man! Right after I pulverize you!" Roger ran toward Doug, who had moved over to the dining room table. Doug dodged the attack. As Roger flew past him, Doug grabbed a dinner bell off the table and rang it quickly.

Getting up, Roger said, "Oh, I see you've finished your cookie. May I get you another?"

"No, thanks," said Doug. "By the way, did you have trouble sleeping the other night?" The doorbell rang.

"Yeah," Roger said, putting Doug in a headlock as he gave him noogies. "What about it?"

Doug rang the bell in his hand and asked, "Did you see that hypnotist's infomercial?"

"Why, yes, as a matter of fact, I did," Roger said, smoothing Doug's hair back into place.

An ice cream truck passed by ringing its bell.

"Shmoudini?" Roger snarled. "I've seen that quack before. That's another reason I should cream you, Funnie! I bought his tapes—I wanted to hypnotize some of you losers at school. But they didn't work at all!" Roger grabbed Doug by the hair.

"I think they worked better than you think," Doug said, ringing the bell again. "Don't you get it, Roger? Every time a bell rings, you're nice, and when it rings again, you're mean. You must have hypnotized yourself with those tapes."

"Well, by all means, let's find out," said Roger politely. "Have another cookie."

Dear Journal,

Just as I thought, Roger had hypnotized himself. He had ordered *How to Hypnotize Your Friends for Fun and Profit*, but Mr. Shmoudini had delivered *Hypnotize Yourself to a Better You*, a self-hypnosis tape! So while Roger thought he was learning how to hypnotize Mr. Bone into being nice to him whenever a bell rang, Roger was actually hypnotizing himself into being nice whenever a bell rang. We

had to call Mr. Shmoudini to unhypnotize Roger, but now everything is back to normal. Except for that quacking thing Roger does whenever a door slams!

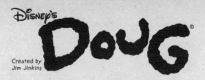

W9-DDJ-106
LunchBox Jokes
Deana Gunn
& Wona Miniati

Lunchbox Jokes: 100 Fun Tear-Out Notes for Kids
by Deana Gunn and Wona Miniati
Designed by Lilla Hangay

Published by Brown Bag Publishers
PO. Box 235065
Encinitas, CA 92023
www.lunchbox-jokes.com

Printed in China by Artron.

ISBN 978-1-938706-13-4

How to Use Lunchbox Jokes:

This book contains 100 tear-out notes, each with a joke. Simply tear out one note, fold it in half (with the question on the outside and the punch line on the inside), and place in your child's lunchbox.

Fold!
Why did the chicken cross the road?
To get to the other side!

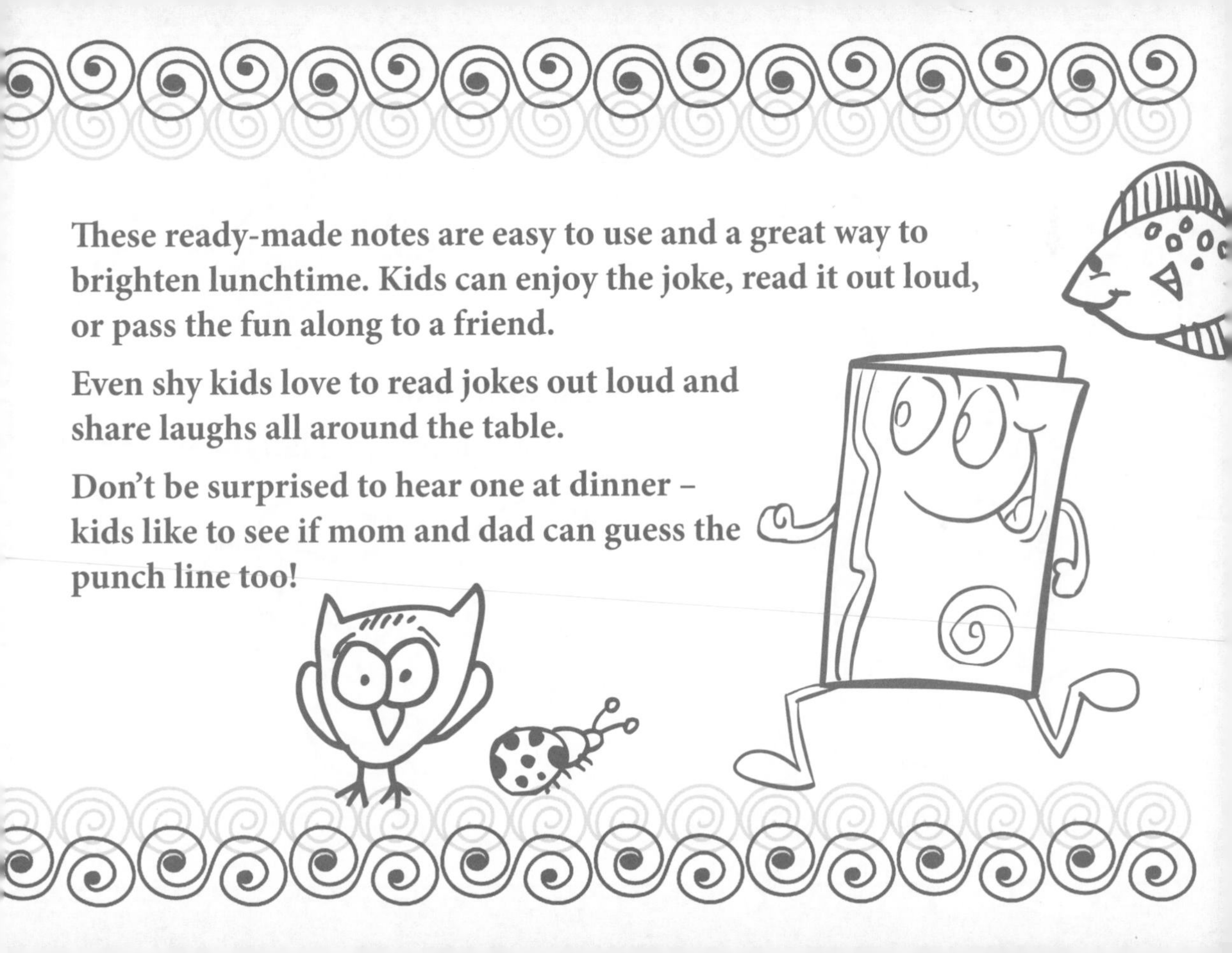

These ready-made notes are easy to use and a great way to brighten lunchtime. Kids can enjoy the joke, read it out loud, or pass the fun along to a friend.

Even shy kids love to read jokes out loud and share laughs all around the table.

Don't be surprised to hear one at dinner – kids like to see if mom and dad can guess the punch line too!

A joke and a punch line
Bring fun to the lunch line
Just tear out a note and fold it in half
Place into the lunchbox for a lunchtime laugh

Lunchbox Jokes
www.lunchbox-jokes.com

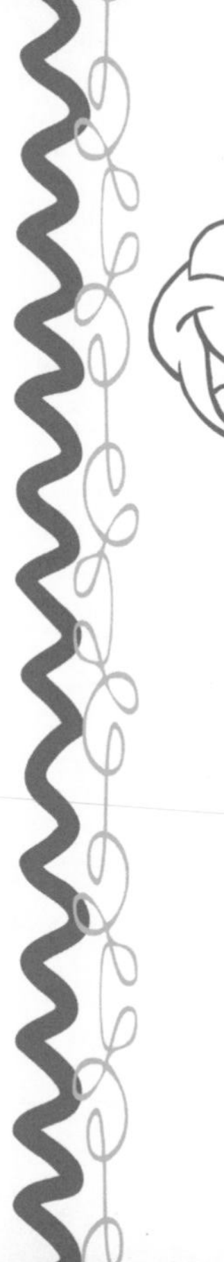

What do you call a song sung in a car?

A car-tune

Lunchbox Jokes
www.lunchbox-jokes.com

What has
2 legs
but can't
walk?

A pair of pants

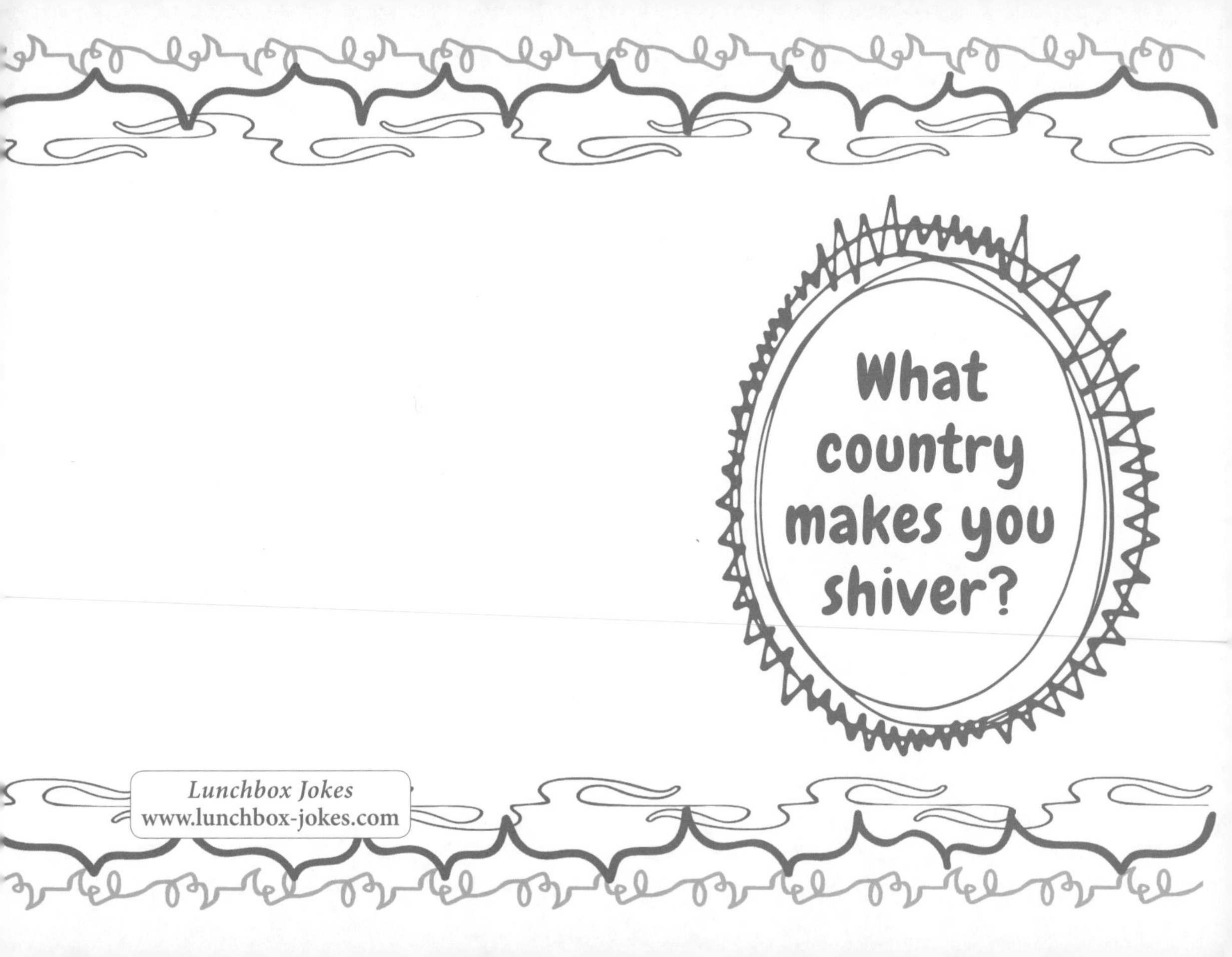
What country makes you shiver?
Lunchbox Jokes
www.lunchbox-jokes.com

Chile

Lunchbox Jokes
www.lunchbox-jokes.com

What has a lot of keys but can't open any doors?

A piano

What did the mother broom say to the baby broom?

It's time to go to sweep

Where do
snowmen go
to dance?

Snow-balls

Lunchbox Jokes
www.lunchbox-jokes.com

What is the longest word in the dictionary?

SMILES
– there
is a mile
between
each S

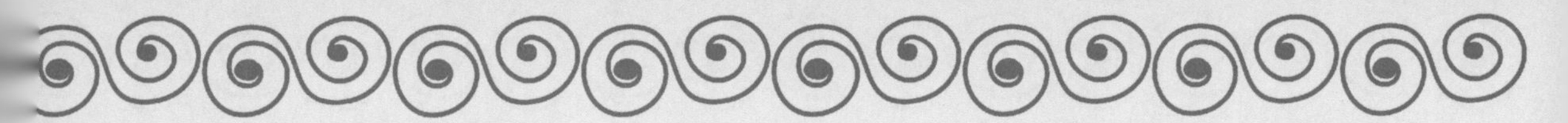

Lunchbox Jokes
www.lunchbox-jokes.com

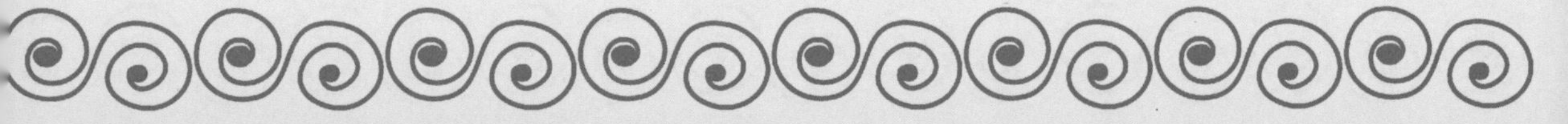

Burple

Why isn't your nose 12 inches long?

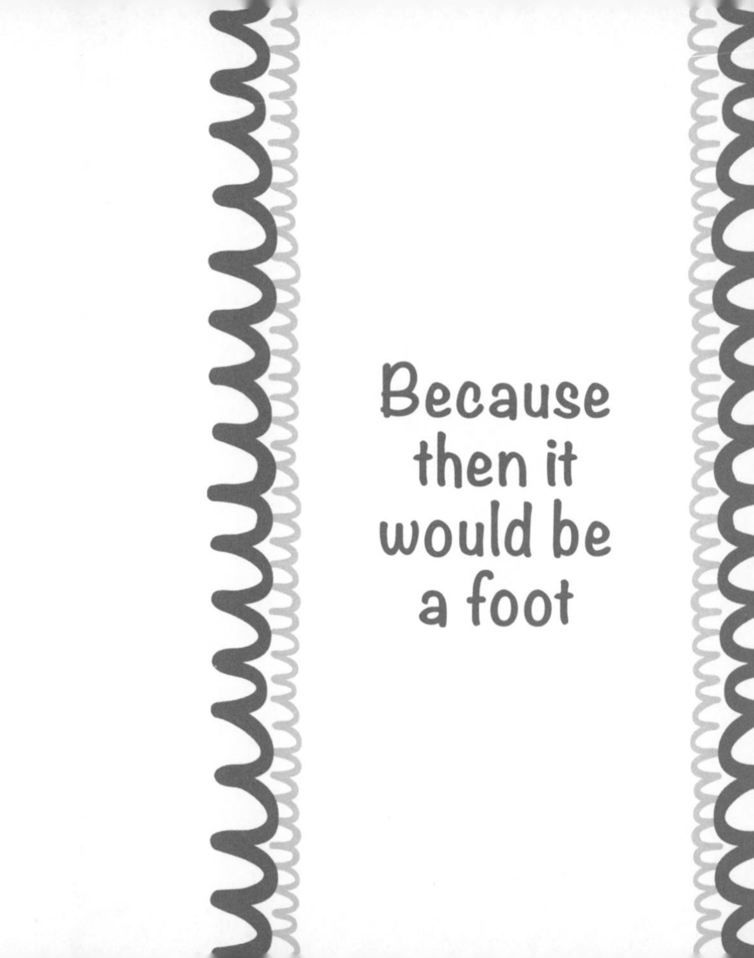
Because
then it
would be
a foot

Lunchbox Jokes
www.lunchbox-jokes.com

Why is
U the
happiest
letter?

Because
it's in the
middle of
FUN

Why was the king too sleepy to win the war?

Too many
late
knights

What did one toilet say to the other toilet?

You look
a bit
flushed

Lunchbox Jokes
www.lunchbox-jokes.com

Why did the boy bring a ladder to school?

He wanted to see what High School was like

Knock, knock!
Who's there?
Eiffel.
Eiffel who?

Eiffel down
the stairs.

Why was 6 afraid of 7?

Because 7 ATE 9

Why don't cannibals eat clowns?
Lunchbox Jokes
www.lunchbox-jokes.com

Because they taste funny

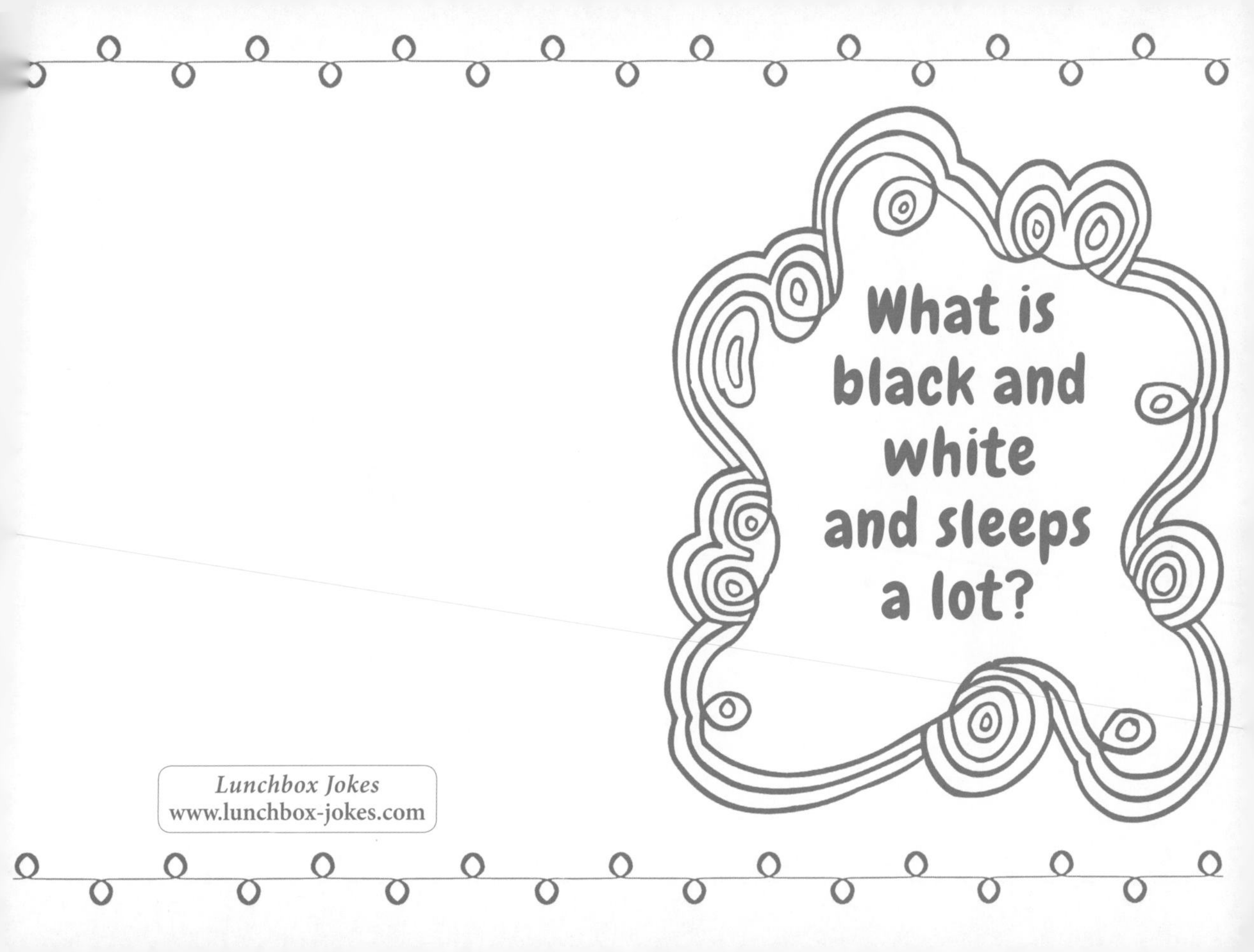
What is black and white and sleeps a lot?
Lunchbox Jokes
www.lunchbox-jokes.com

A snooze-paper

Lunchbox Jokes
www.lunchbox-jokes.com

What do you call a fairy that doesn't take baths?

Stinkerbell

How do you
make seven
an even
number?

Take the
s out

Lunchbox Jokes
www.lunchbox-jokes.com

Why are ghosts bad liars?

Because you can see right through them

Lunchbox Jokes
www.lunchbox-jokes.com

What has 4 legs but can't walk?

A chair

What did one math book say to the other math book?

Boy, do
I have
problems

Why did the kid sleep with a ruler?

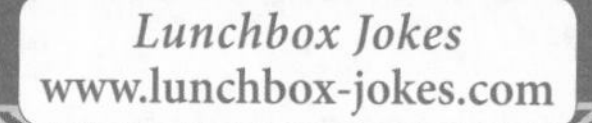

To measure
how long
he slept

Lunchbox Jokes
www.lunchbox-jokes.com

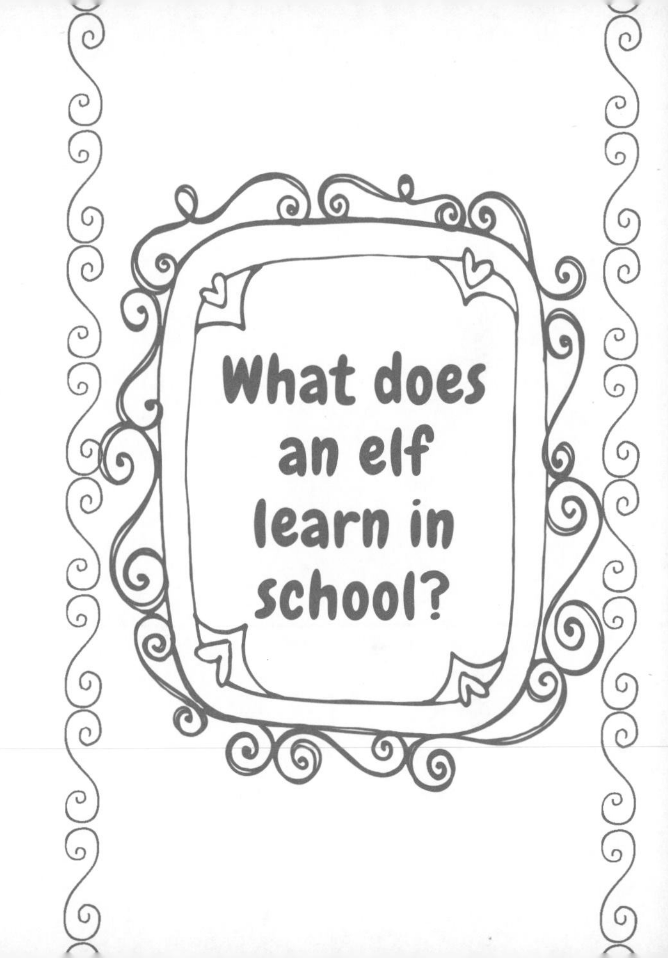
What does an elf learn in school?

The
elf-abet

Lunchbox Jokes
www.lunchbox-jokes.com

Why did the house go to the doctor?

Because
he had
window
panes

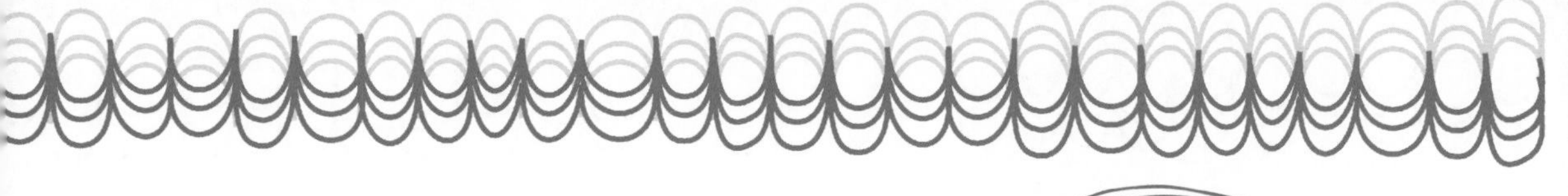

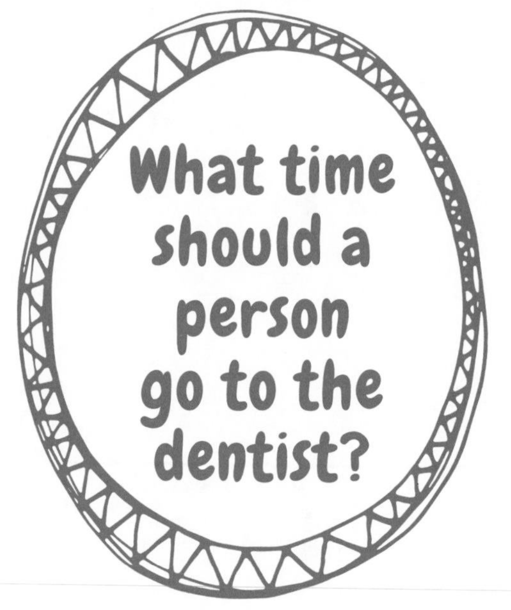
What time
should a
person
go to the
dentist?

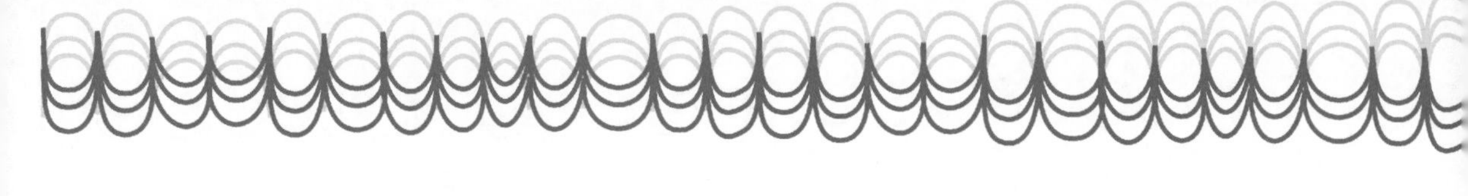

At tooth-
hurty

What did the computer do at lunchtime?

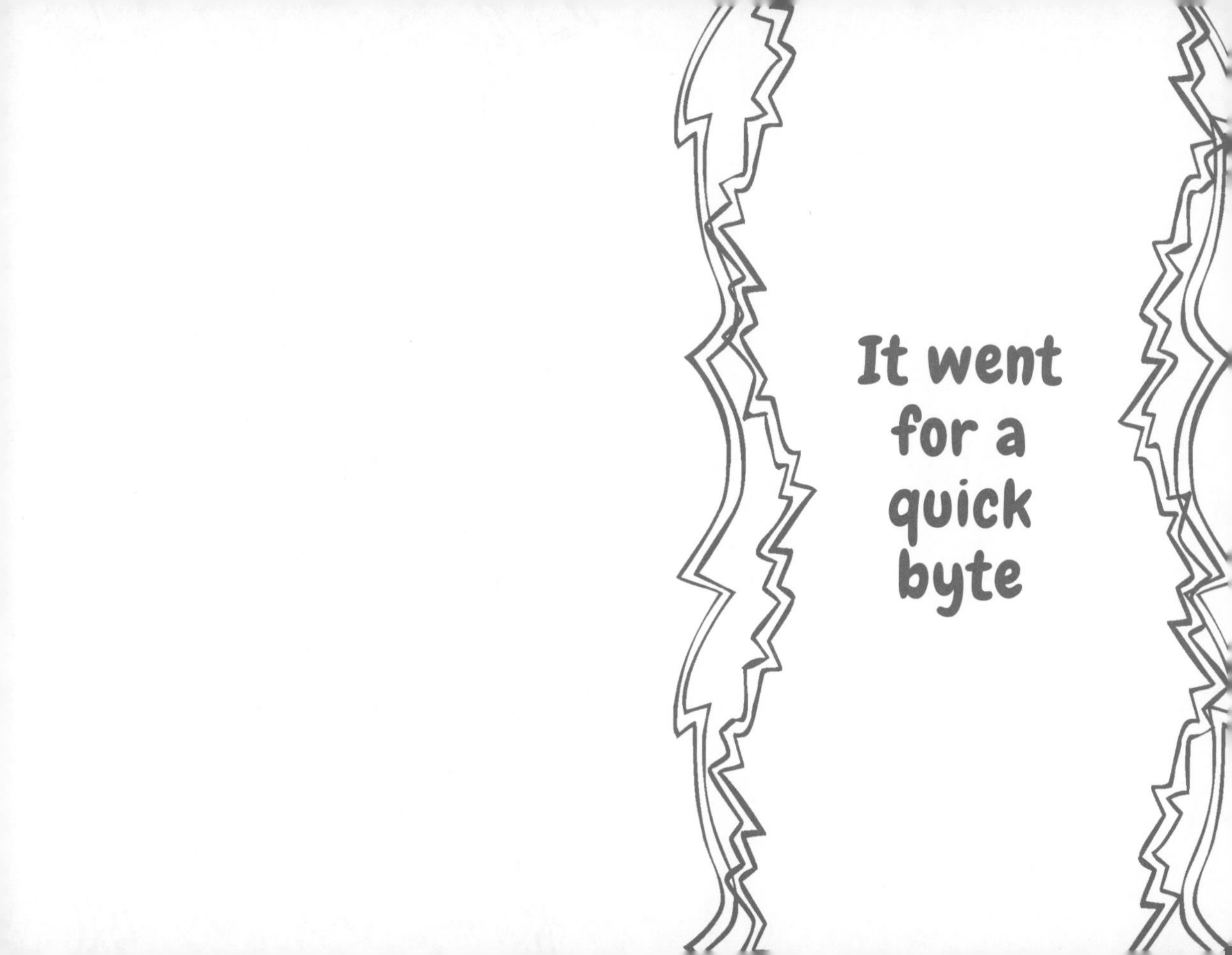
It went
for a
quick
byte

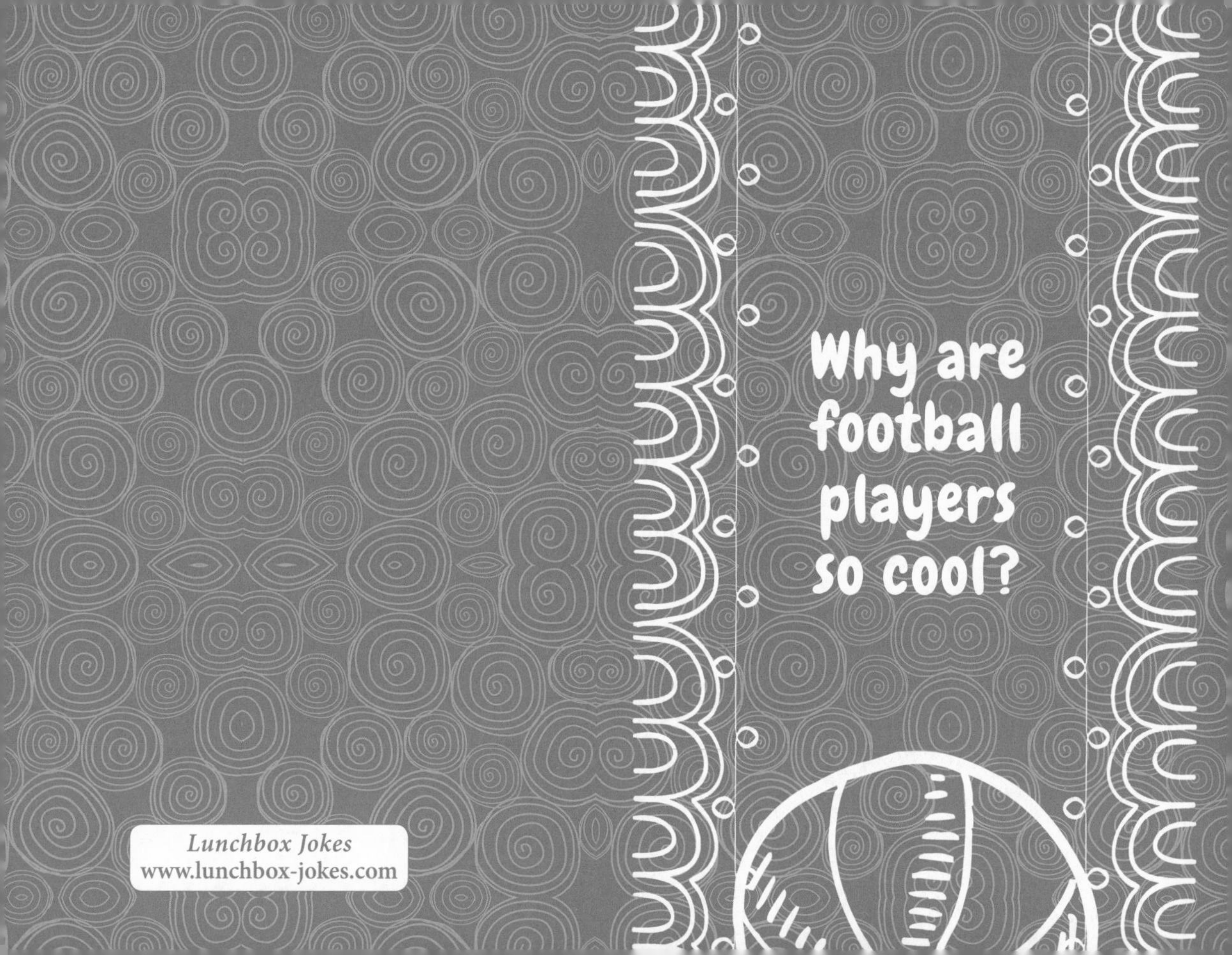
Lunchbox Jokes
www.lunchbox-jokes.com
Why are football players so cool?

Because
they have
fans

What has
a head, a
tail, and
no body?

A coin

Lunchbox Jokes
www.lunchbox-jokes.com

Knock,
knock!
Who's there?
Waddle.
Waddle
who?

Waddle you do if I don't let you in?

Why was
the skeleton
laughing?
Lunchbox Jokes
www.lunchbox-jokes.com

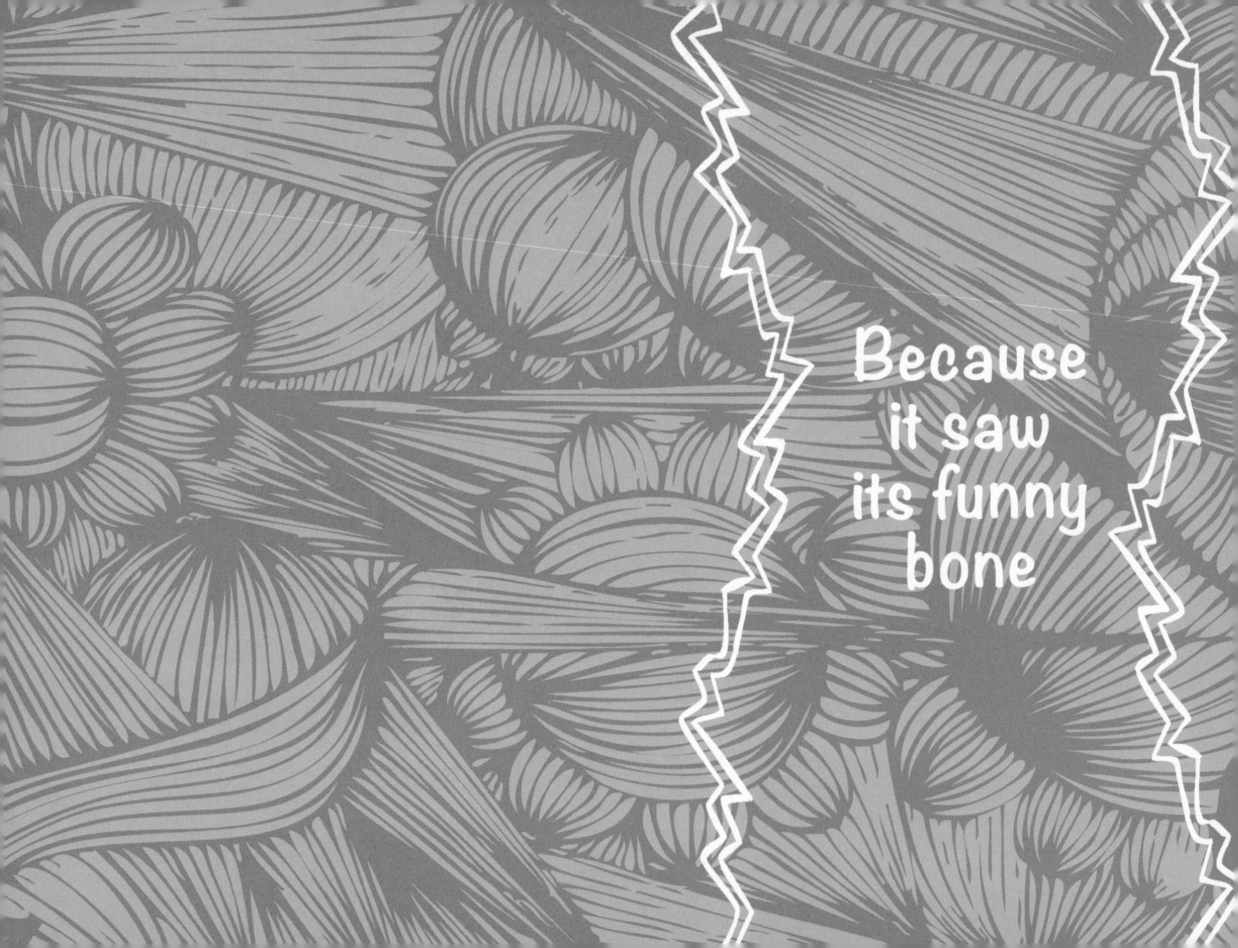
Because
it saw
its funny
bone

Why did Mickey Mouse go to outer space?

Because he wanted to see Pluto

What kind of glasses does a ghost wear?

Spook-tacles

Why did the computer go to the doctor?

Because it
had a virus

Why don't
you do math
in a jungle?

If you add 4+4 you get ATE

What has 4 wheels and flies?

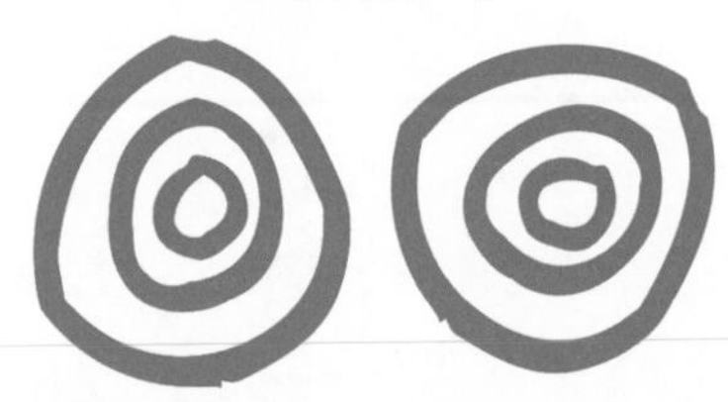

A garbage truck

Where do you wash a vampire?

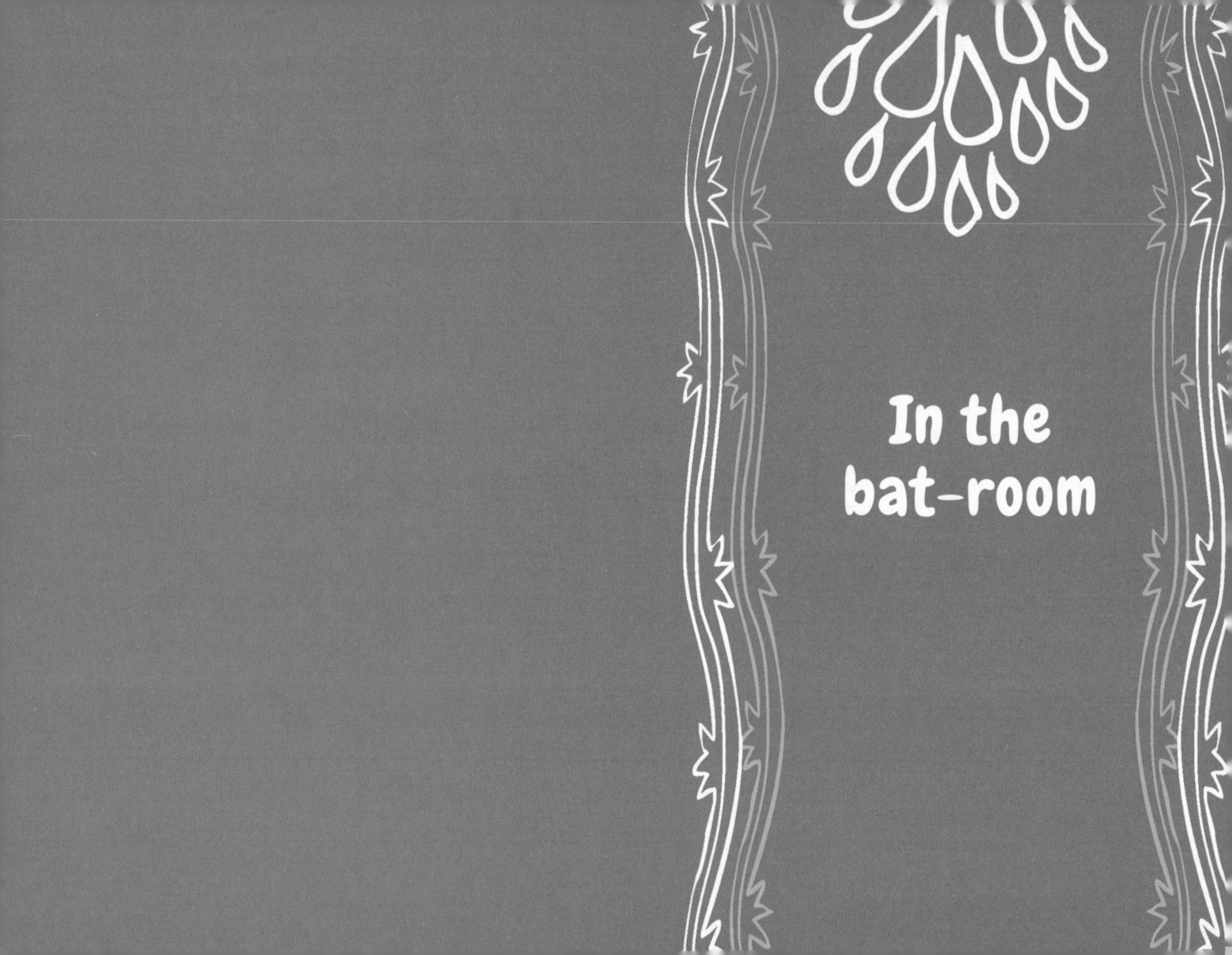

In the bat-room

Knock knock!
Who's there?
Ya.
Ya who?

You don't
have to cheer;
it's only a
knock-knock
joke.

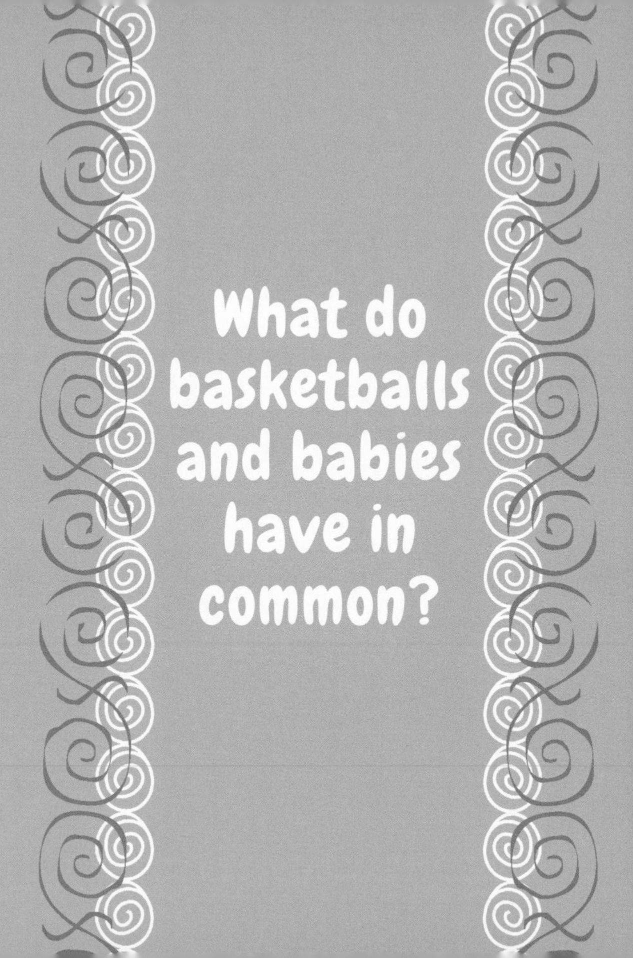
What do
basketballs
and babies
have in
common?

They both dribble

Lunchbox Jokes
www.lunchbox-jokes.com

What
is the
tallest
building?

A library
because it
has the most
stories

Lunchbox Jokes
www.lunchbox-jokes.com

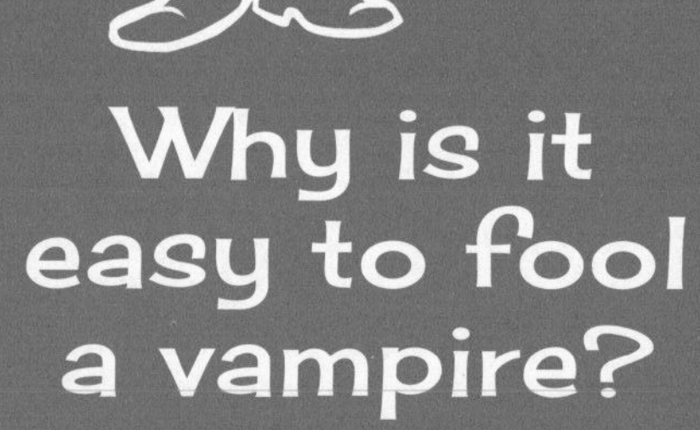
Why is it
easy to fool
a vampire?

Because they are suckers

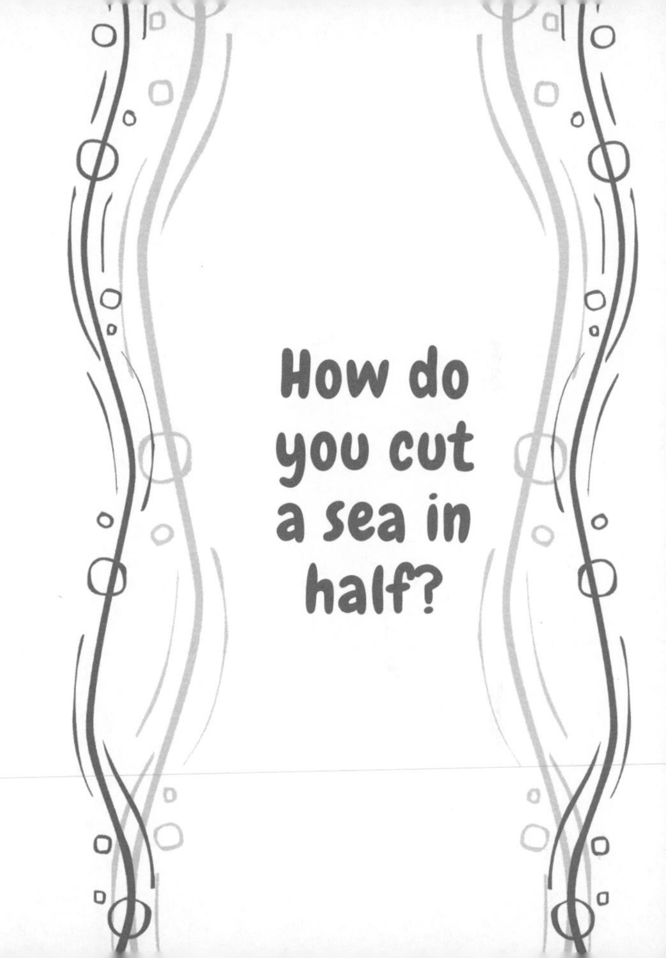
How do you cut a sea in half?

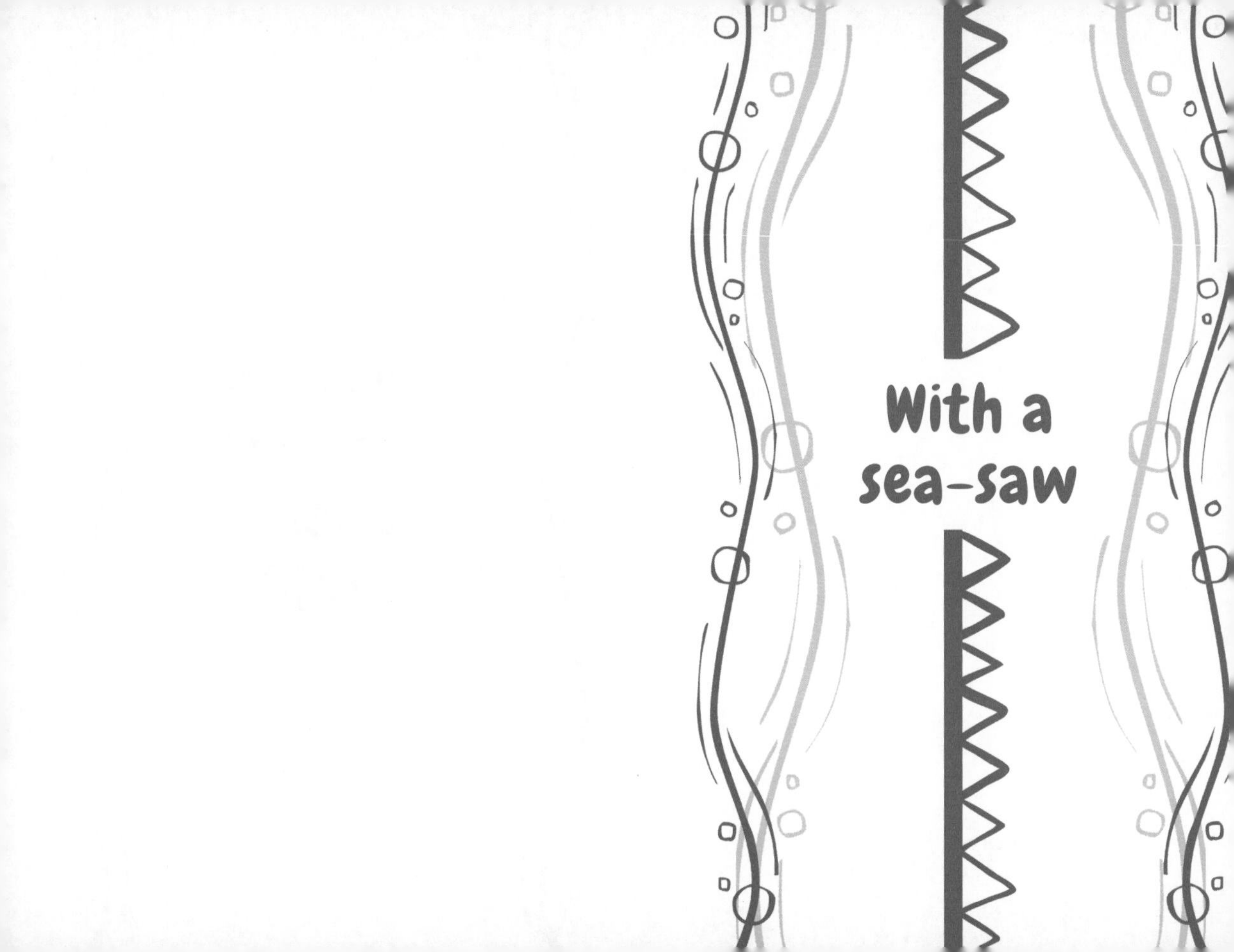
With a
sea-saw

Lunchbox Jokes
www.lunchbox-jokes.com

Knock, knock!
Who's there?
Pasture.
Pasture who?

Pasture
bedtime!
Go to bed!

What starts with T, ends with T, and is full of T?

A teapot

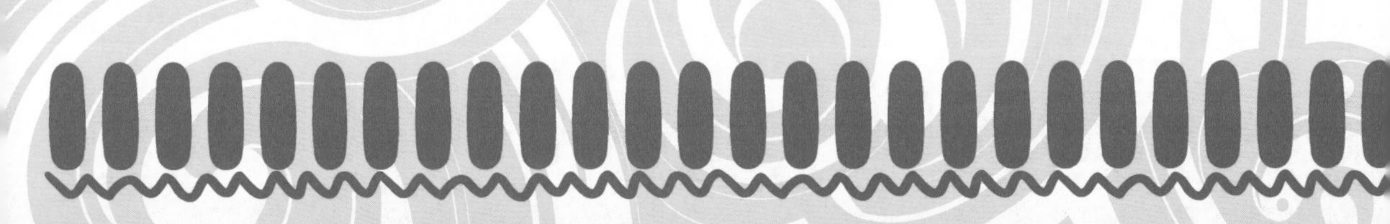

Why did the car have a stomach ache?

He had too
much gas

What kind of star goes to jail?

A shooting
star

Lunchbox Jokes
www.lunchbox-jokes.com

Why
did the
basketball
player
go to the
doctor?

To get
more
shots

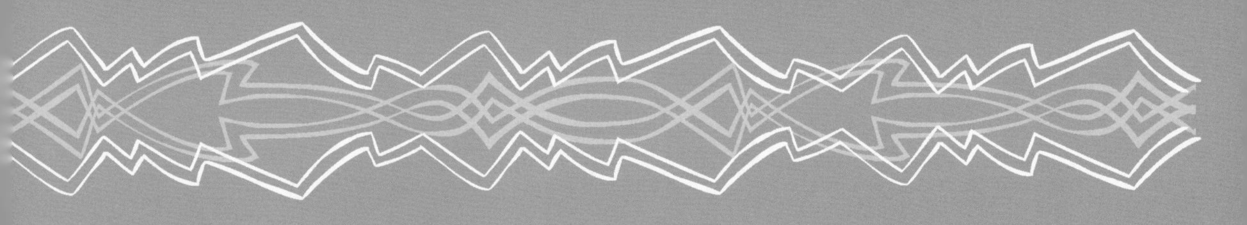

Knock knock!
Who's there?
Icing.
Icing who?

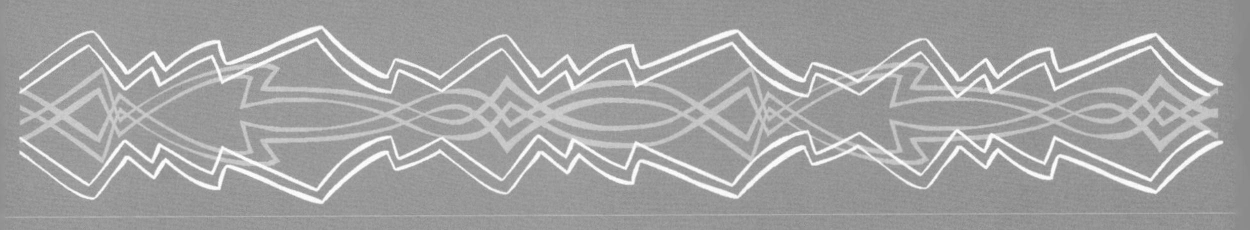

Icing in
the choir.
Do you?

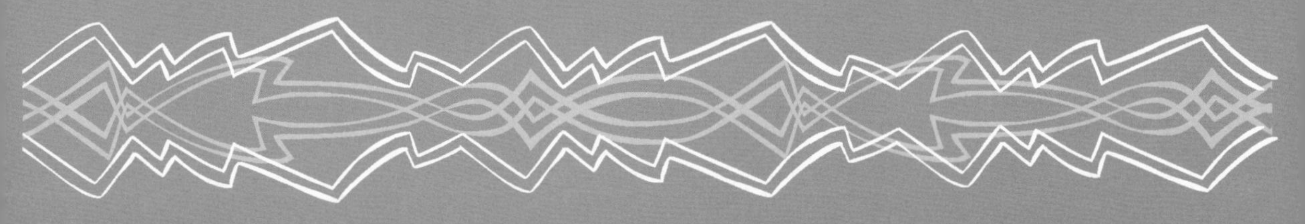

Why did the boy bring home a chair from school?

Because the teacher told him to please take a seat

Knock, knock!
Who's there?
Police!
Police who?

Lunchbox Jokes
www.lunchbox-jokes.com

Police let us in, it's cold out here!

Why did the boy take a leash into a thunderstorm?

It was raining
cats and dogs

Lunchbox Jokes
www.lunchbox-jokes.com

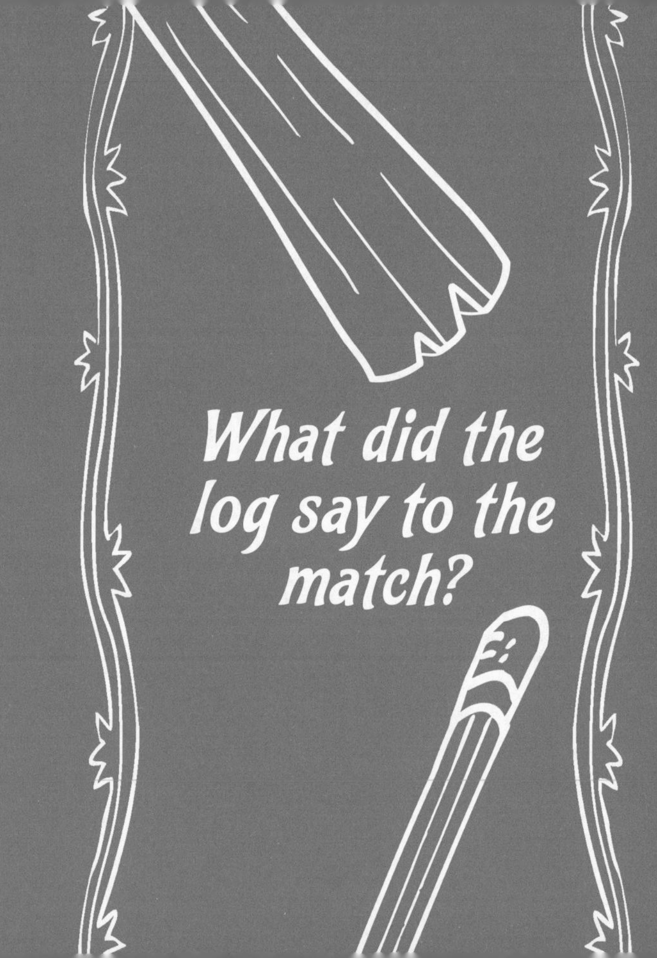
What did the log say to the match?

You burn
me up

What do you get when you bake stones with your bread dough?

Lunchbox Jokes
www.lunchbox-jokes.com

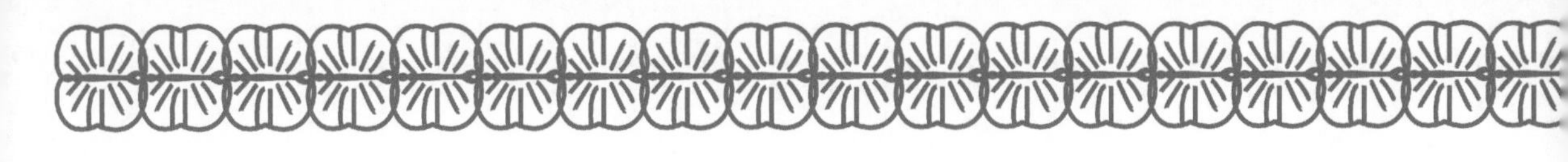

Rock-n-roll

Lunchbox Jokes
www.lunchbox-jokes.com

Why did the baseball player go to jail?

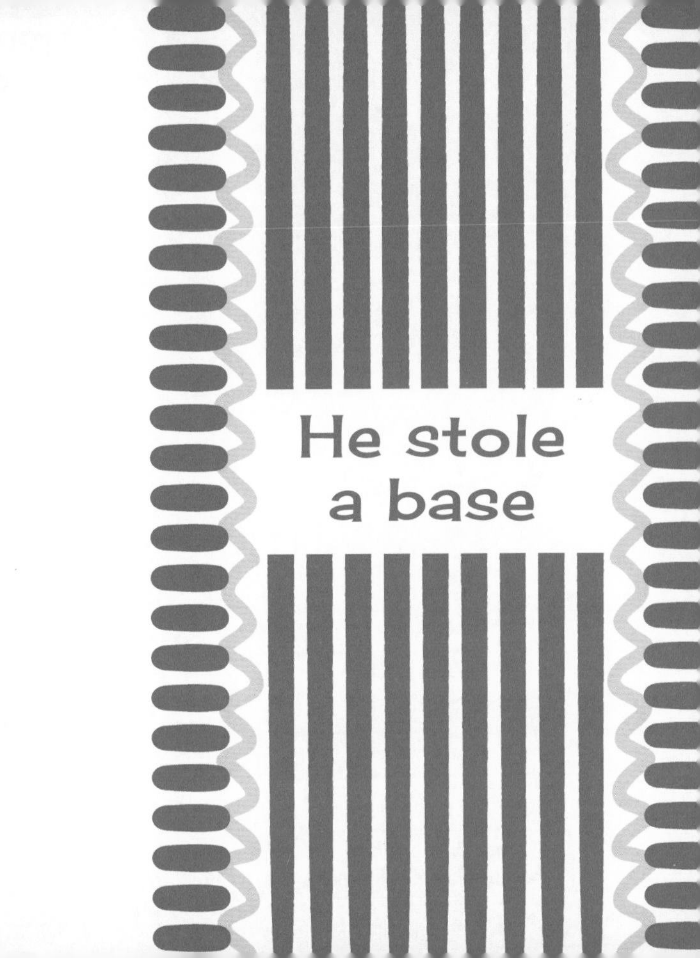
He stole
a base

Knock knock!
Who's there?
Hawaii.
Hawaii who?

Lunchbox Jokes
www.lunchbox-jokes.com

I'm fine,
Hawaii you?

Why did the computer go to the store?

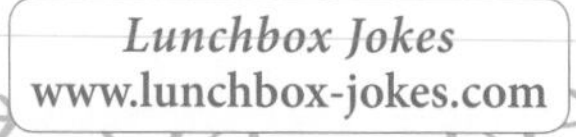

To buy
some chips

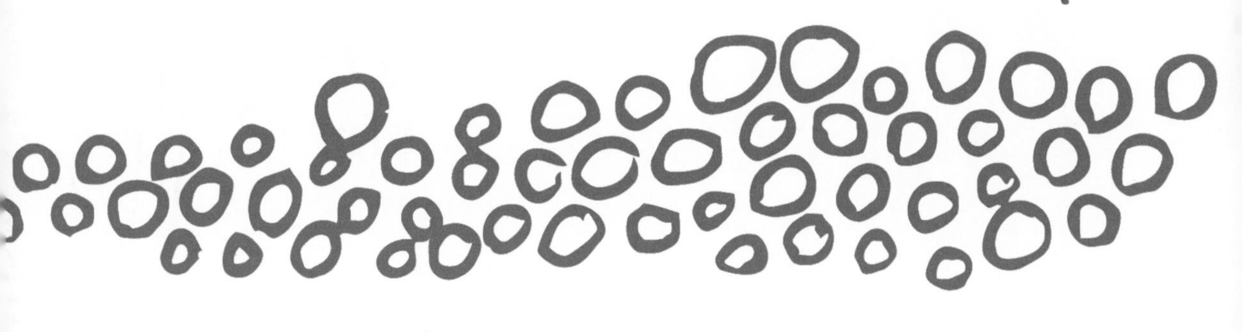

Why couldn't the pirate play cards?
Lunchbox Jokes
www.lunchbox-jokes.com

He was standing on the deck

Why
are twin
witches
hard
to tell
apart?
Lunchbox Jokes
www.lunchbox-jokes.com

They can't
tell witch
is witch

Why are bowlers bad baseball players?

They're always getting strikes

Lunchbox Jokes
www.lunchbox-jokes.com

What did the policeman say to his tummy?

You're
under a
vest!

Knock,
knock!
Who's
there?
Tank.
Tank
who?
Lunchbox Jokes
www.lunchbox-jokes.com

You're
welcome!

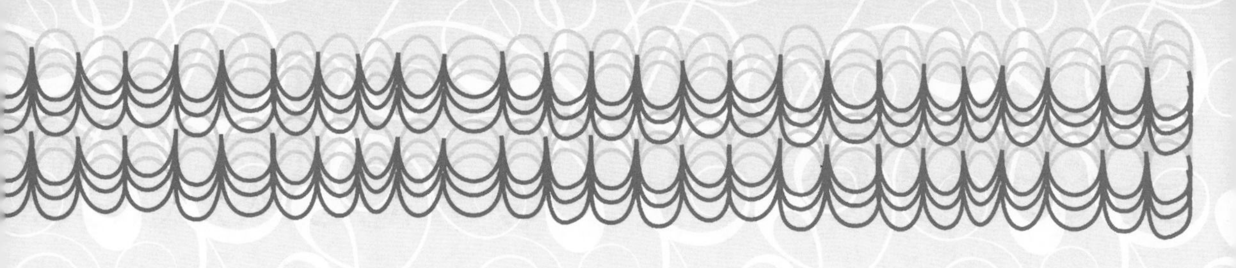

Which state has a ton of laundry to do?

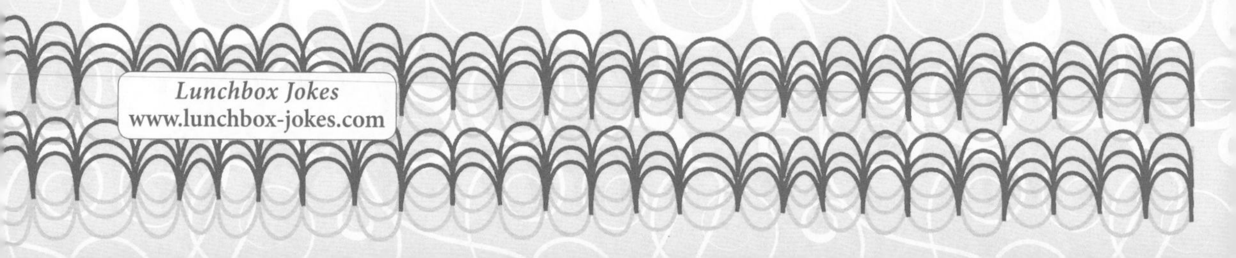

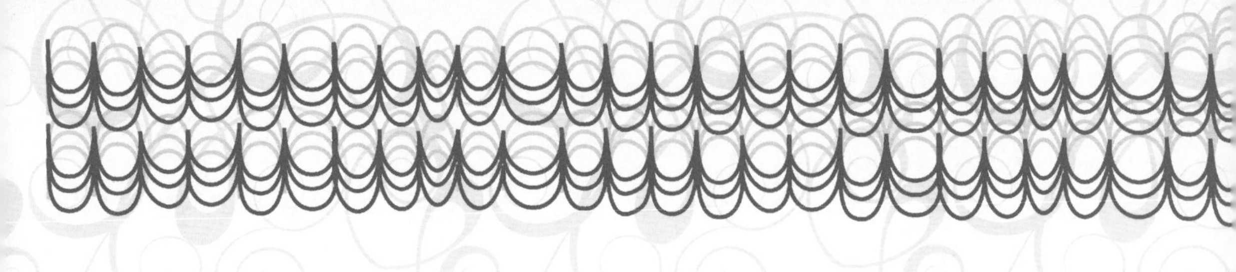

Washington

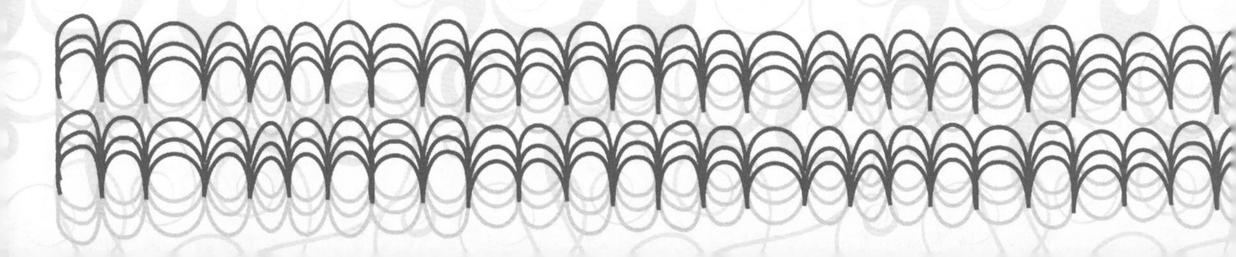

Knock
knock!
Who's
there?
Ash.
Ash who?

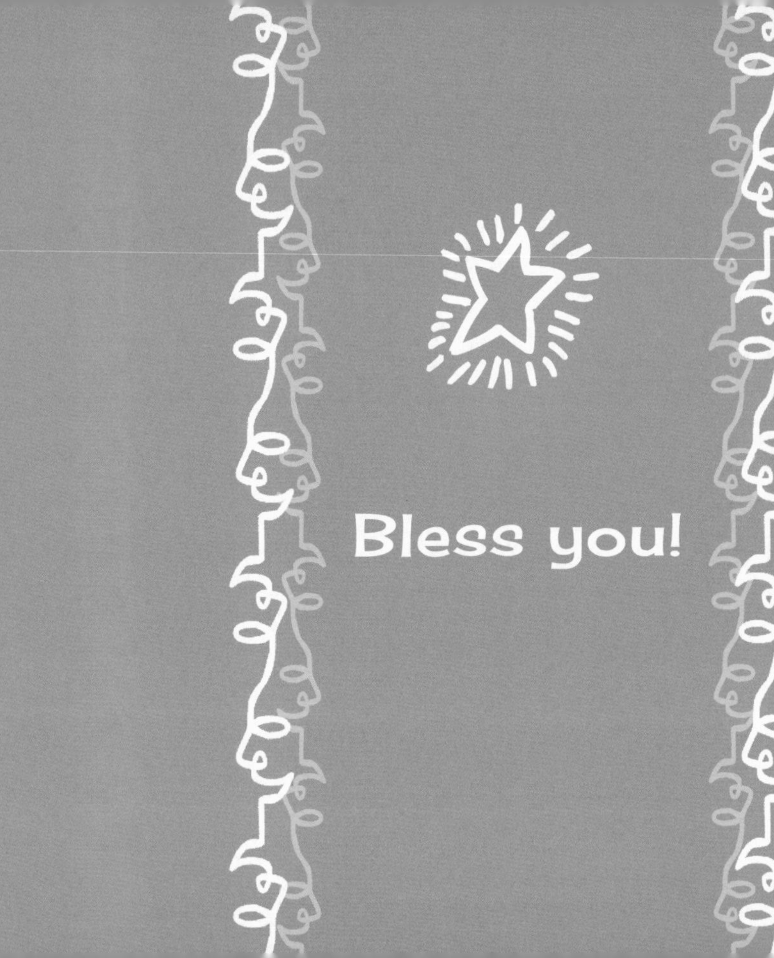
Bless you!

What was wrong with the wooden car?

It wooden go

What runs around the yard without moving?

A fence

Why are dragons bad bosses?
Lunchbox Jokes
www.lunchbox-jokes.com

They keep on firing people

Lunchbox Jokes
www.lunchbox-jokes.com

Where do computers go to dance?

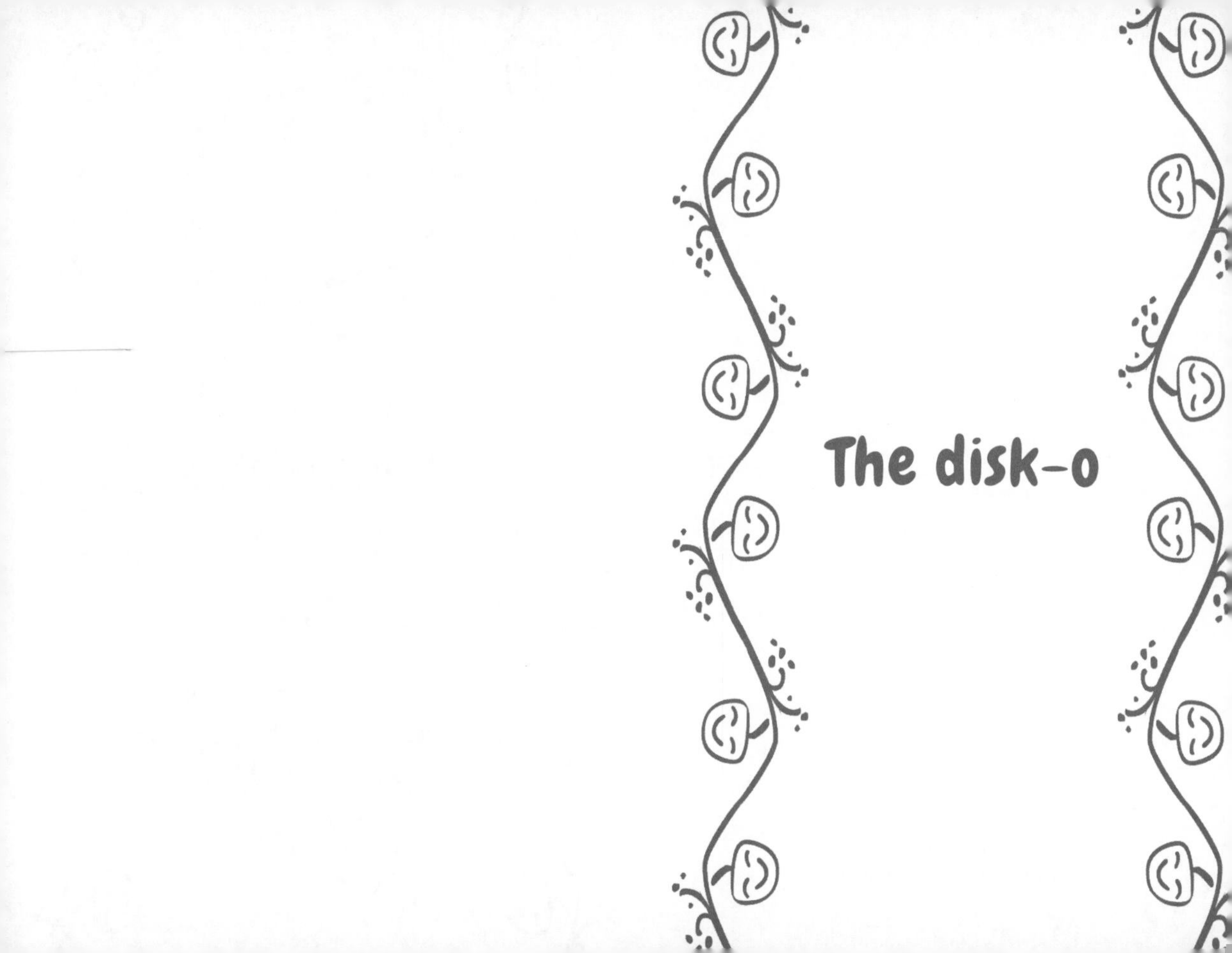

The disk-o

What kind of music do mummies like?
Lunchbox Jokes
www.lunchbox-jokes.com

Wrap

Knock knock!
Who's there?
Snow.
Snow who?

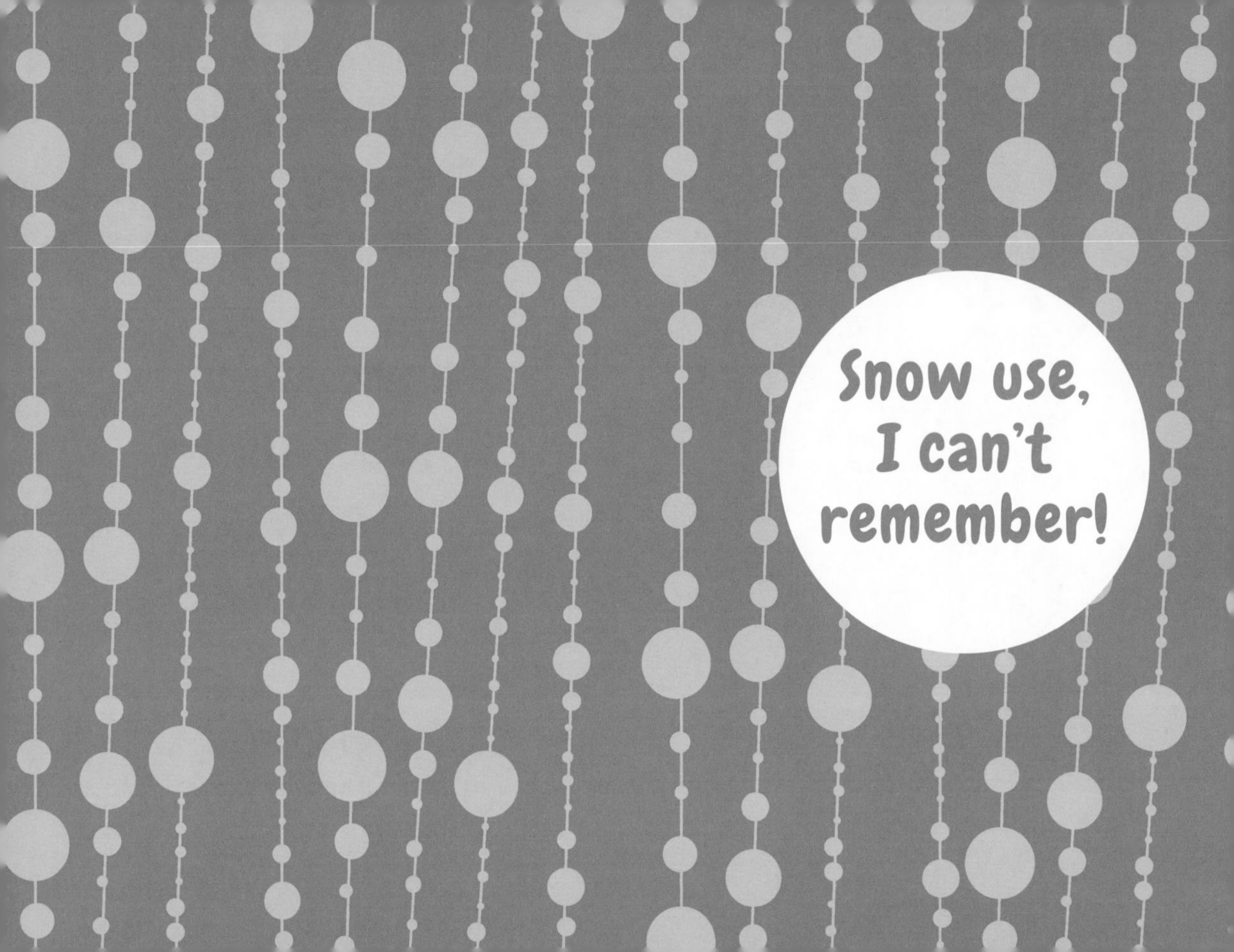
Snow use,
I can't
remember!

Why didn't the 11-year old get into the pirate movie?

It was
rated
ARRRR!

What kind of phones do they use in prison?

Cell phones

Lunchbox Jokes
www.lunchbox-jokes.com

Why do
cats love
computers?

Because
they come
with a
mouse

Why did the boy put his report card over his head?

He
wanted
to get
higher
grades

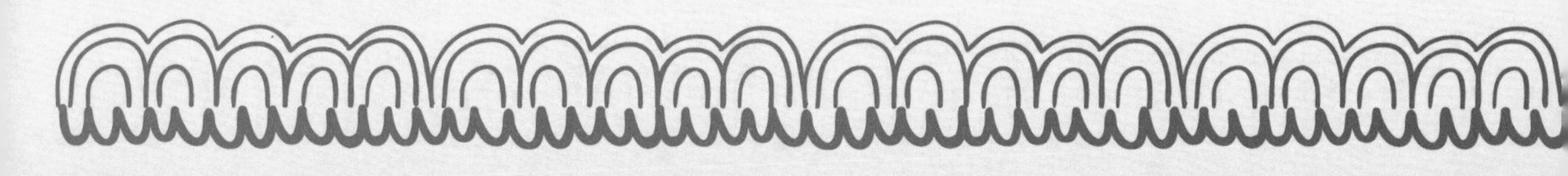

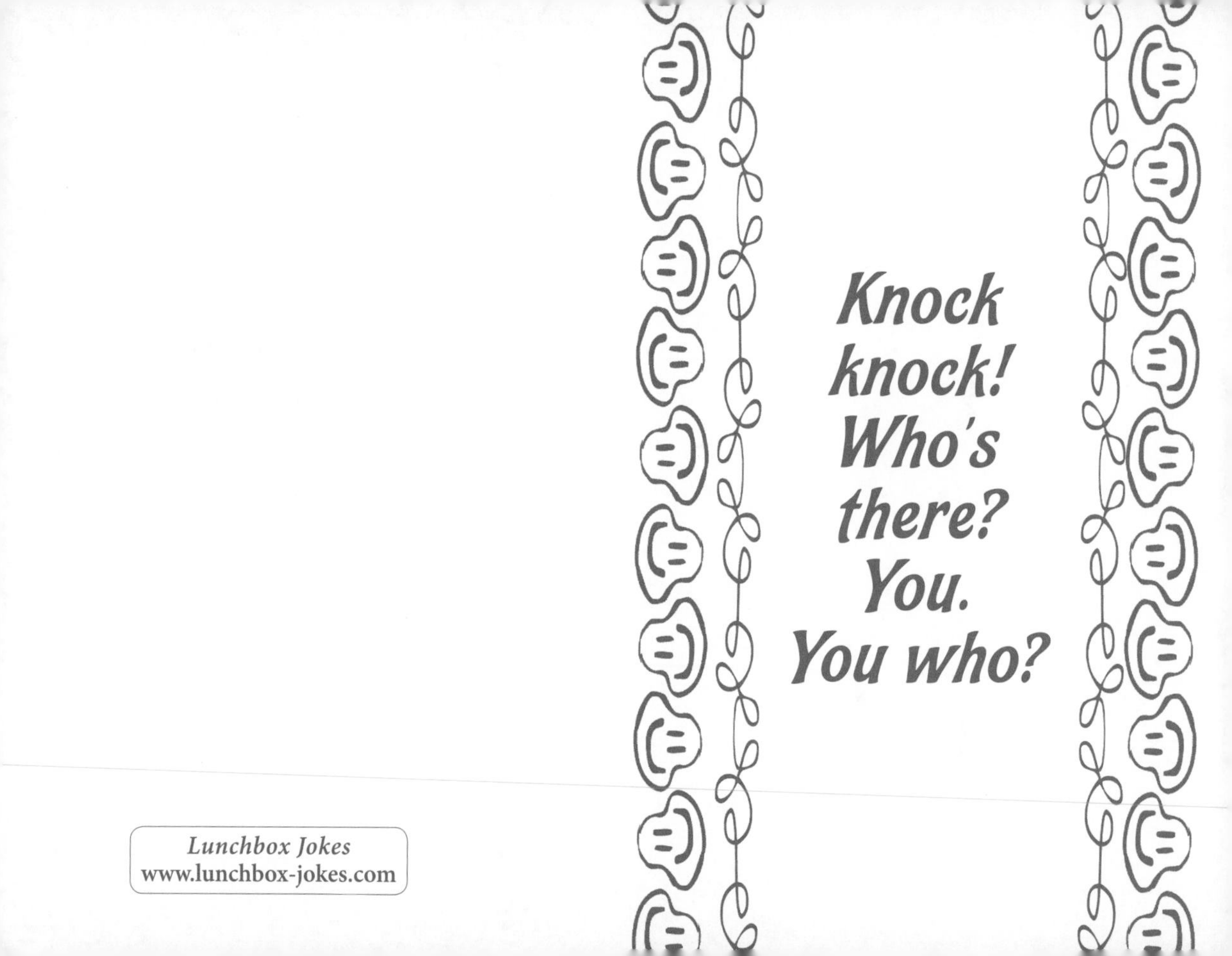
Knock
knock!
Who's
there?
You.
You who?
Lunchbox Jokes
www.lunchbox-jokes.com

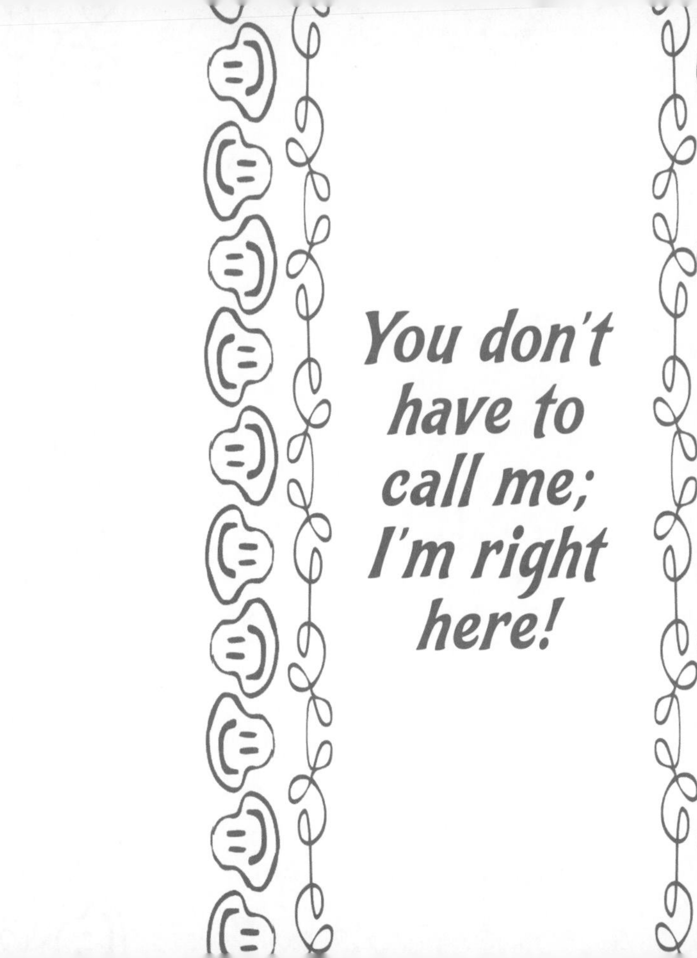
You don't
have to
call me;
I'm right
here!

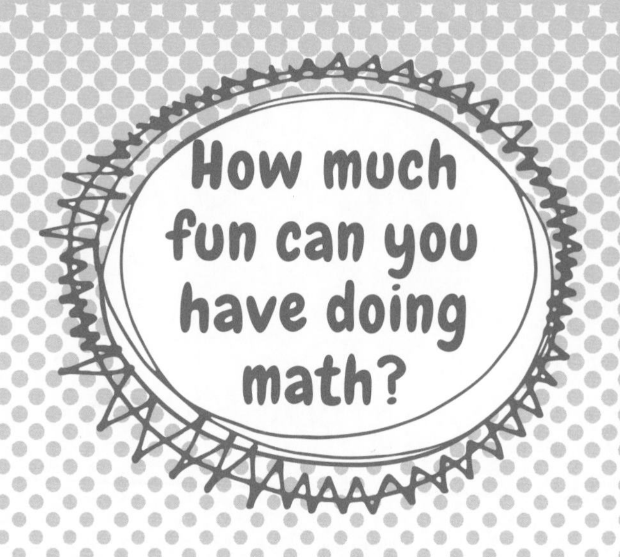
How much fun can you have doing math?

Sum fun

Lunchbox Jokes
www.lunchbox-jokes.com

What do you use to fix a broken tooth?

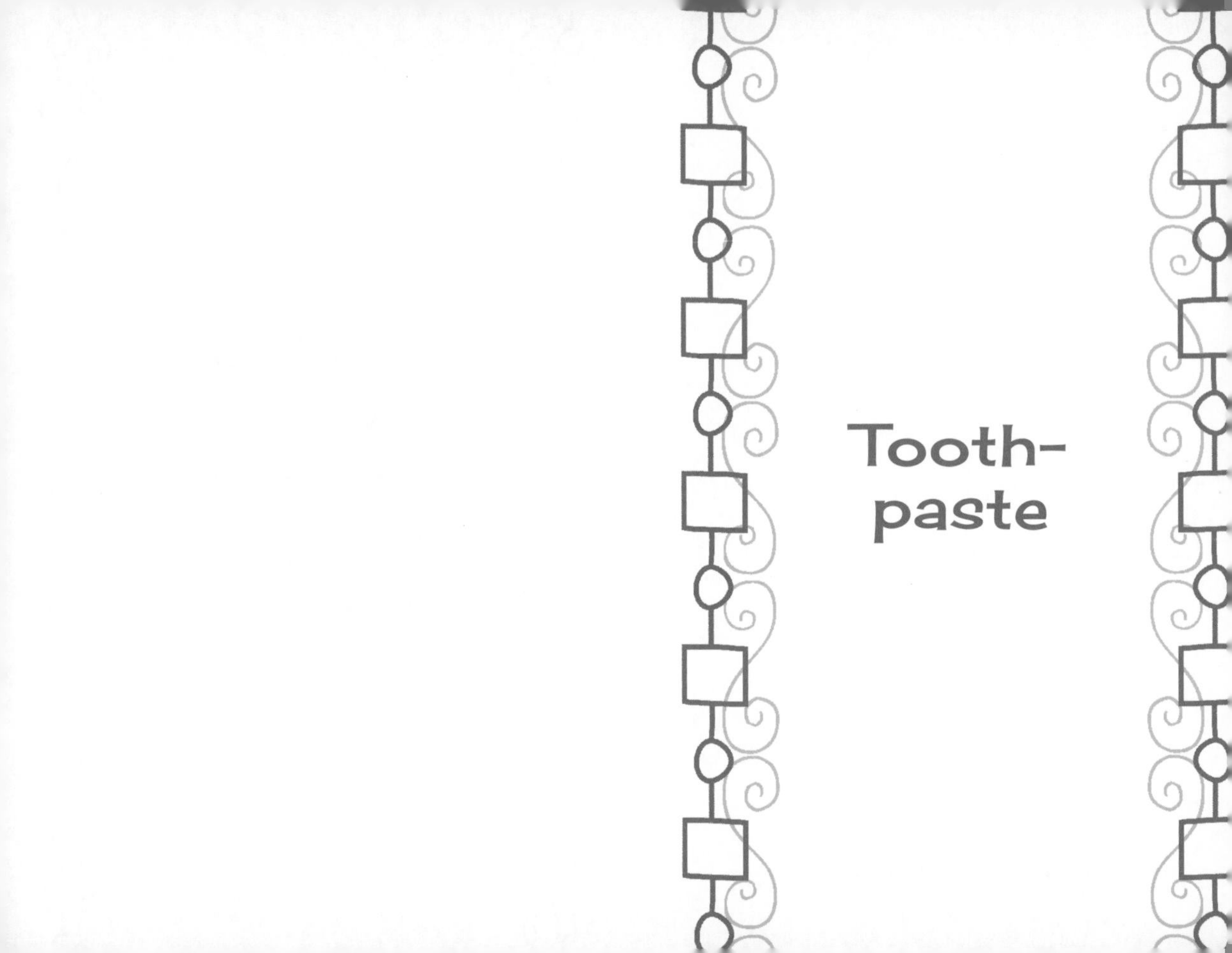

Tooth-paste

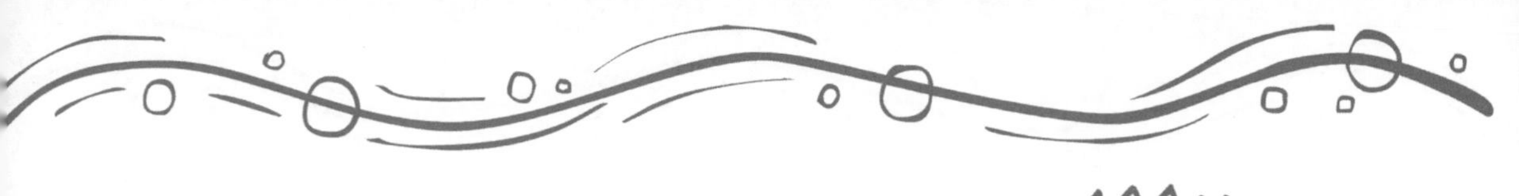

What does a surfer say when he gets married?

I dude

Knock knock!
Who's there?
Disguise.
Disguise who?

Disguise beginning to bug me!

Why didn't the skeleton cross the road?

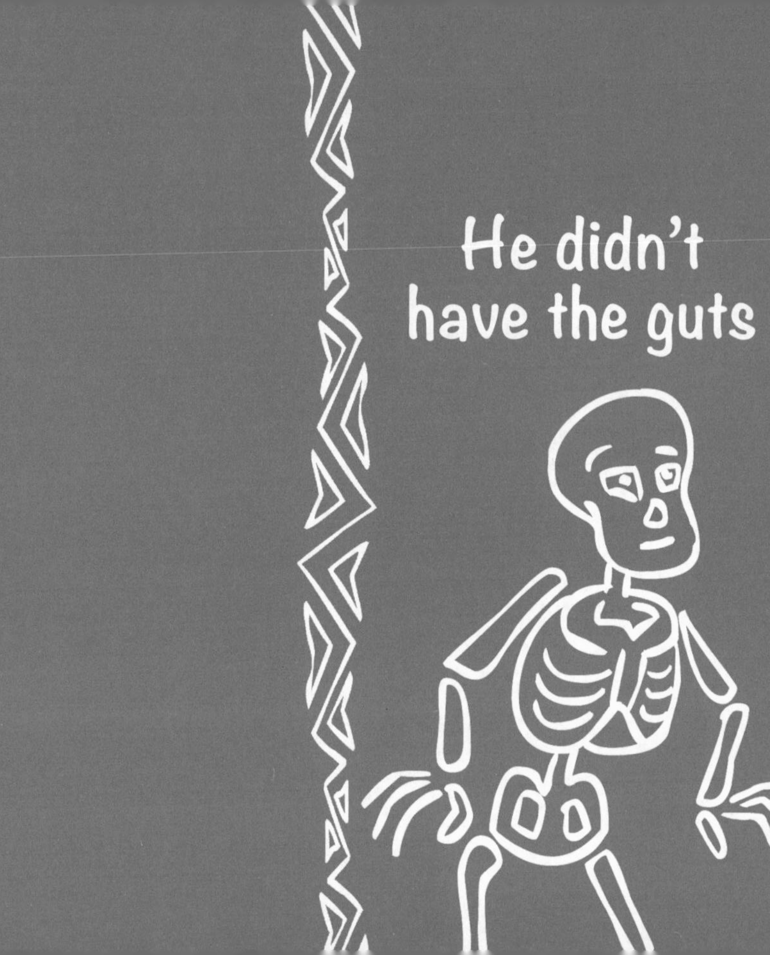
He didn't
have the guts

What did the beach say when the tide finally came in?

Long time
no sea

Lunchbox Jokes
www.lunchbox-jokes.com

What kind of nails should a carpenter never hit?

His fingernails

Lunchbox Jokes
www.lunchbox-jokes.com

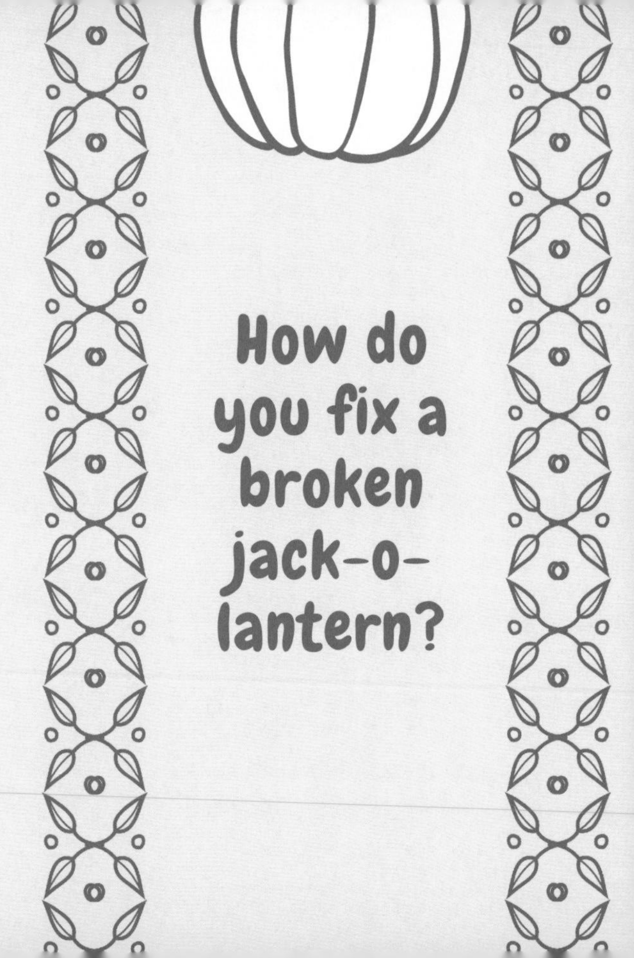

How do you fix a broken jack-o-lantern?

With a
pumpkin
patch

What did the blanket say to the bed?
Lunchbox Jokes
www.lunchbox-jokes.com

I've got you covered

What do
planets
like to
read?

Comet
books

Knock
knock!
Who's
there?
Canoe.
Canoe
who?

Canoe tell
knock-
knock
jokes too?

Knock knock!
Who's there?
Ice cream.
Ice cream who?

Ice cream
at scary
movies.
Do you?

Lunchbox Jokes
www.lunchbox-jokes.com

What do you get if you cross a snowman with a shark?

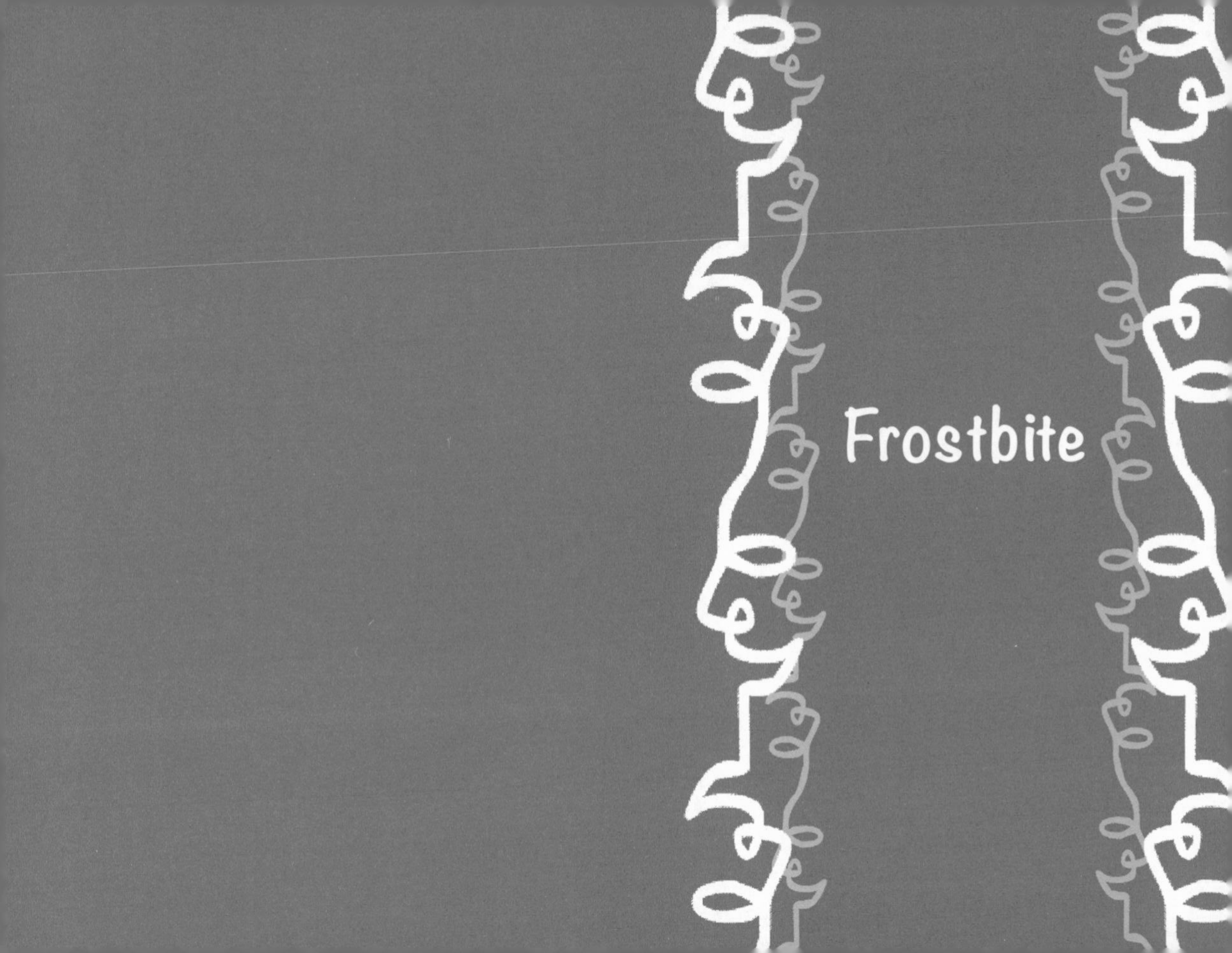
Frostbite

What do you call it when burglars go surfing?

A crime wave

What did one eye say to the other eye?

Something
between us
smells

What kind
of flowers
should you
not give on
Valentine's
Day?

Lunchbox Jokes
www.lunchbox-jokes.com

Cauliflowers

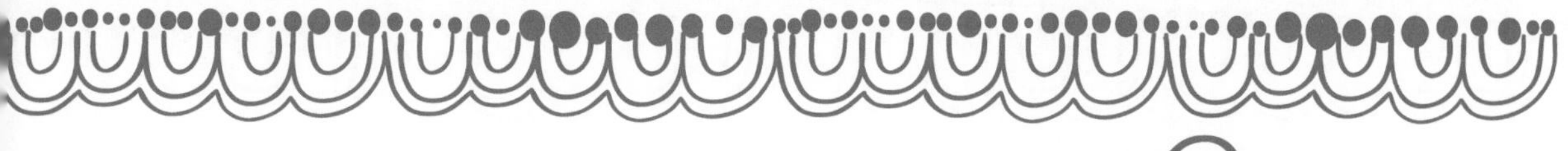

What do you feed a teddy bear?

Nothing –
It's already
stuffed

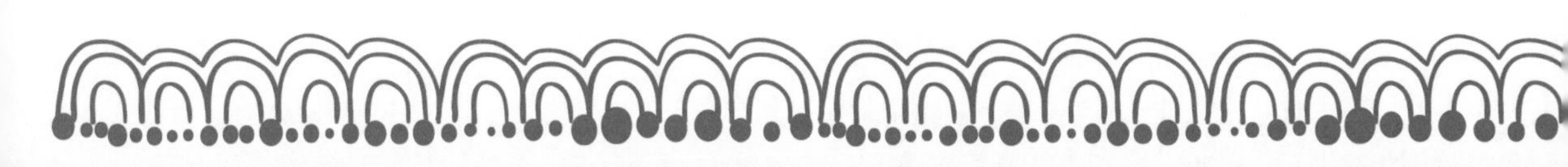

What happens when you annoy a clock?

It gets ticked off

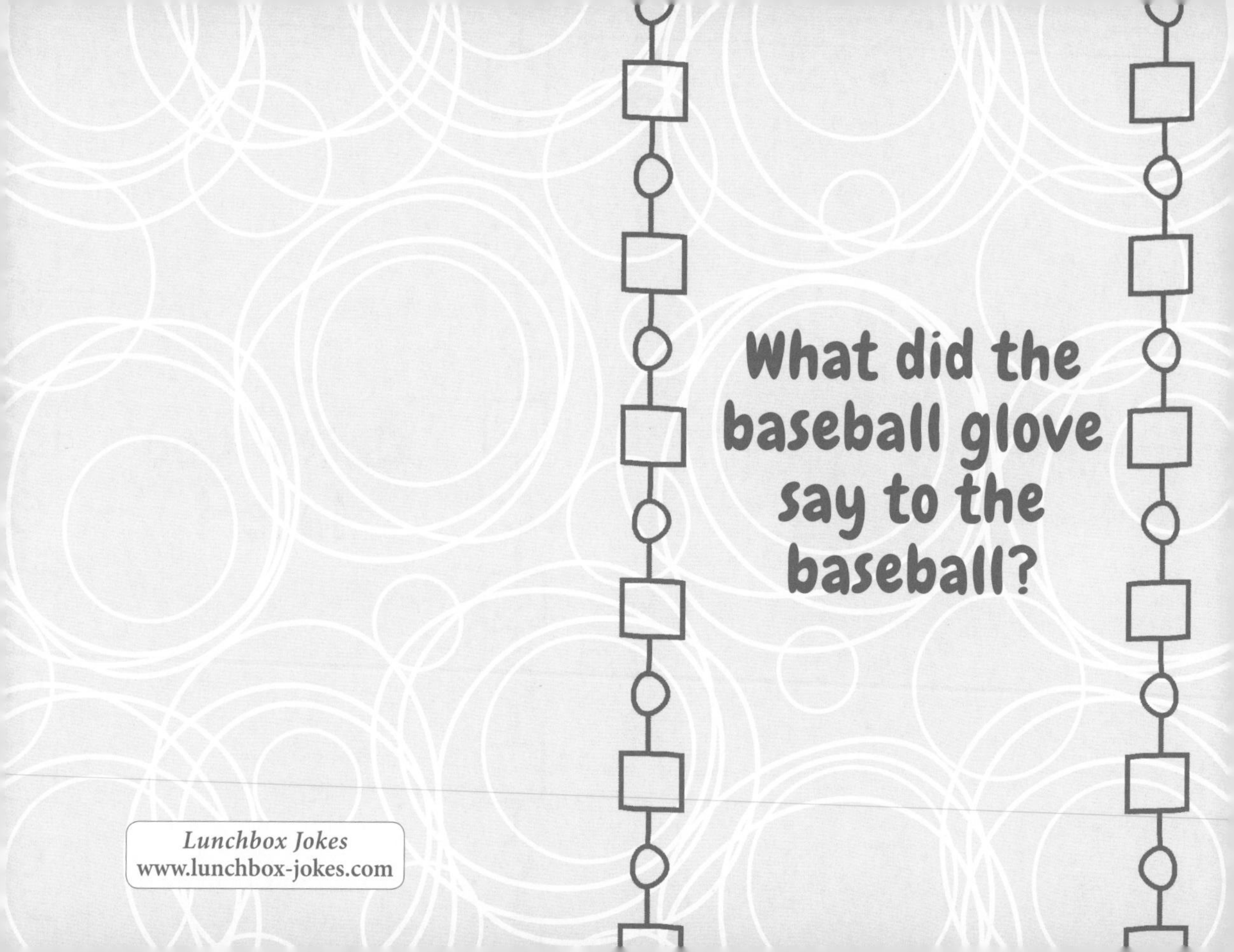
Lunchbox Jokes
www.lunchbox-jokes.com
What did the baseball glove say to the baseball?

Catch you later!

What do you get when you cross a banana with a shoe?

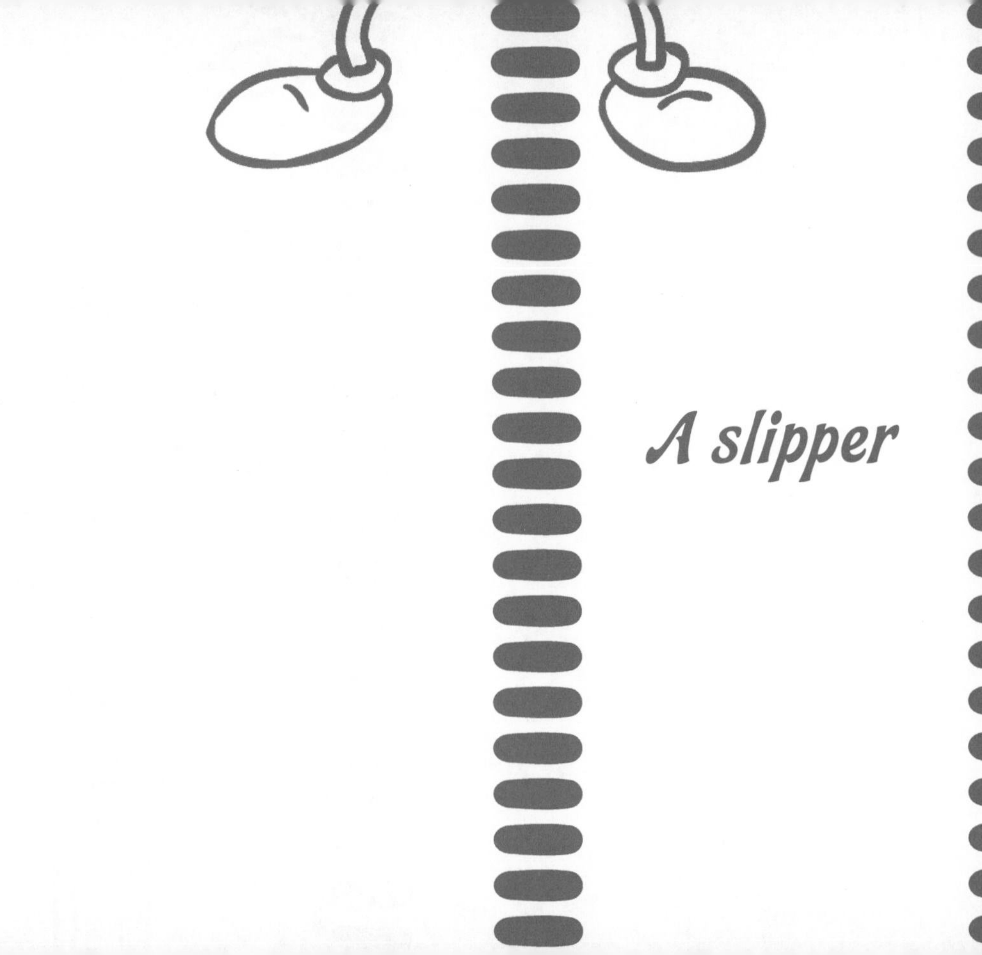
A slipper

What kind of plates do they use in space?

Flying saucers

What do you call a computer superhero?

A screen
saver

Why did the
teacher wear
sunglasses?

Because
her
students
were so
bright

Lunchbox Jokes
www.lunchbox-jokes.com

What does lightning put on during a storm?

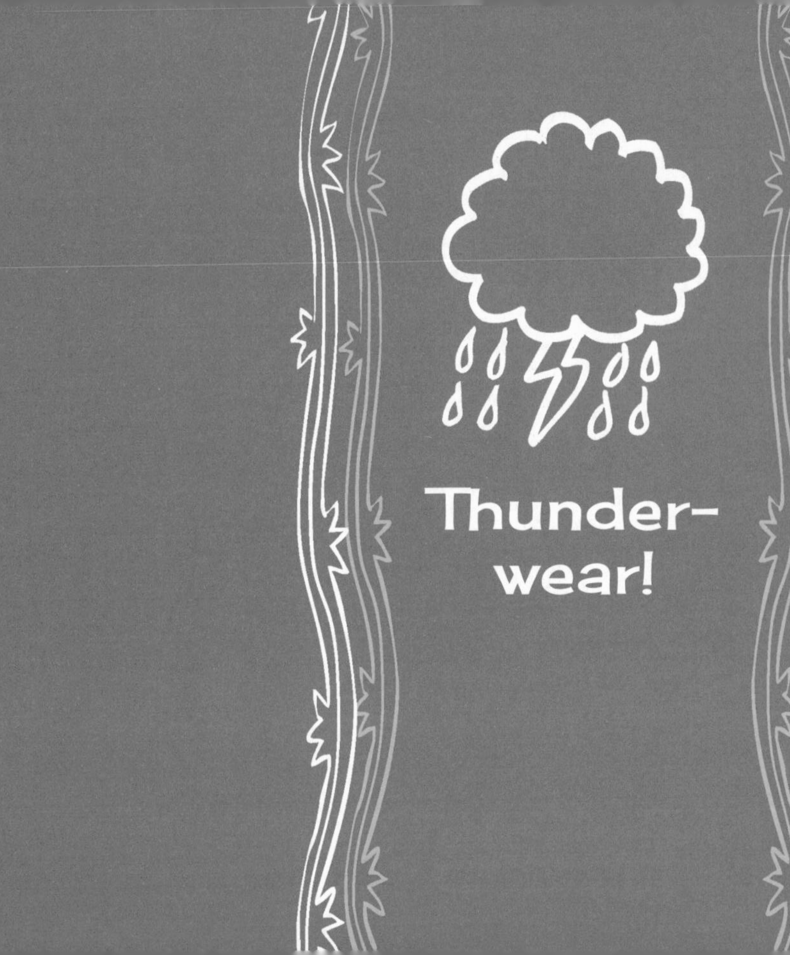
Thunder-
wear!

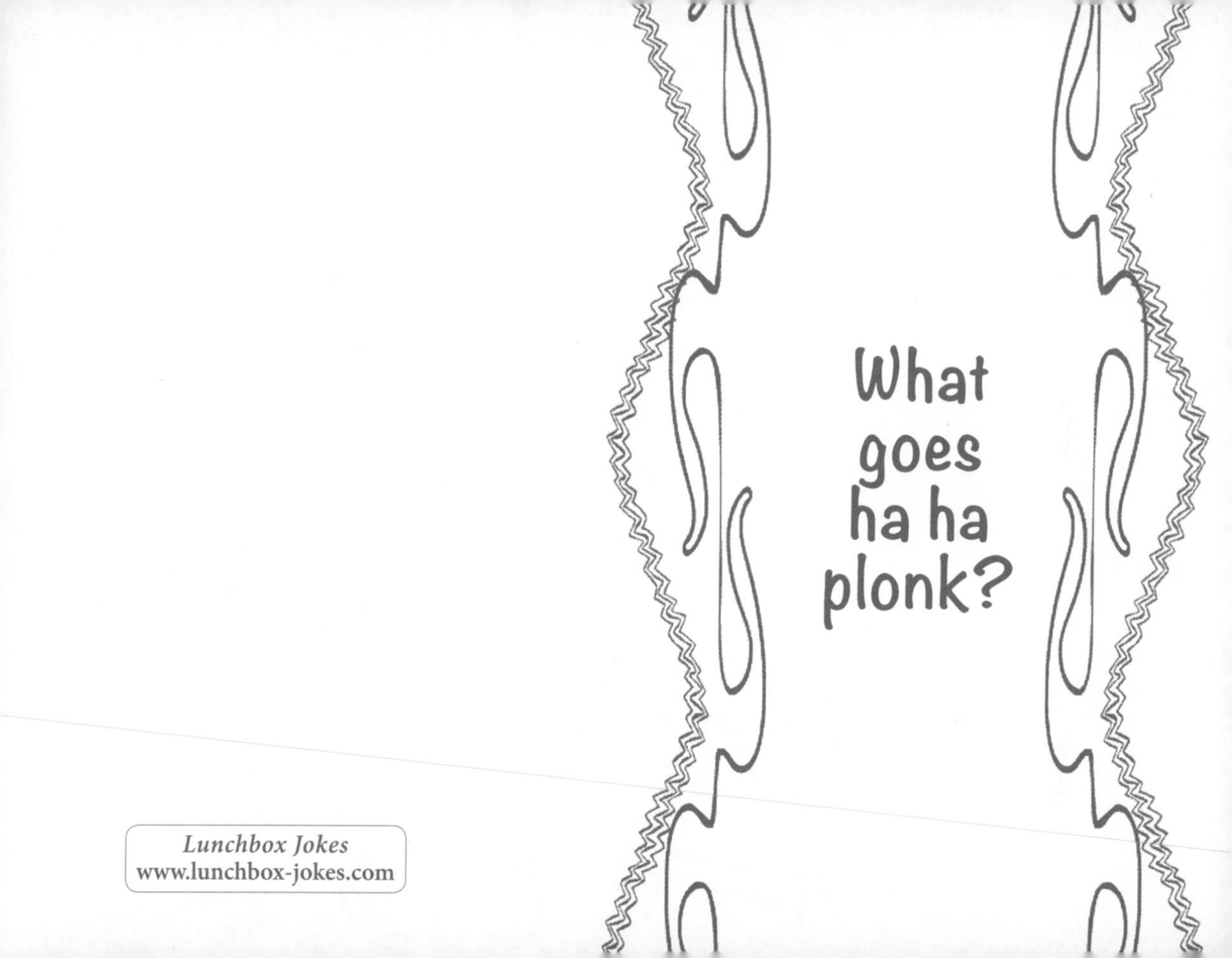
What goes ha ha plonk?

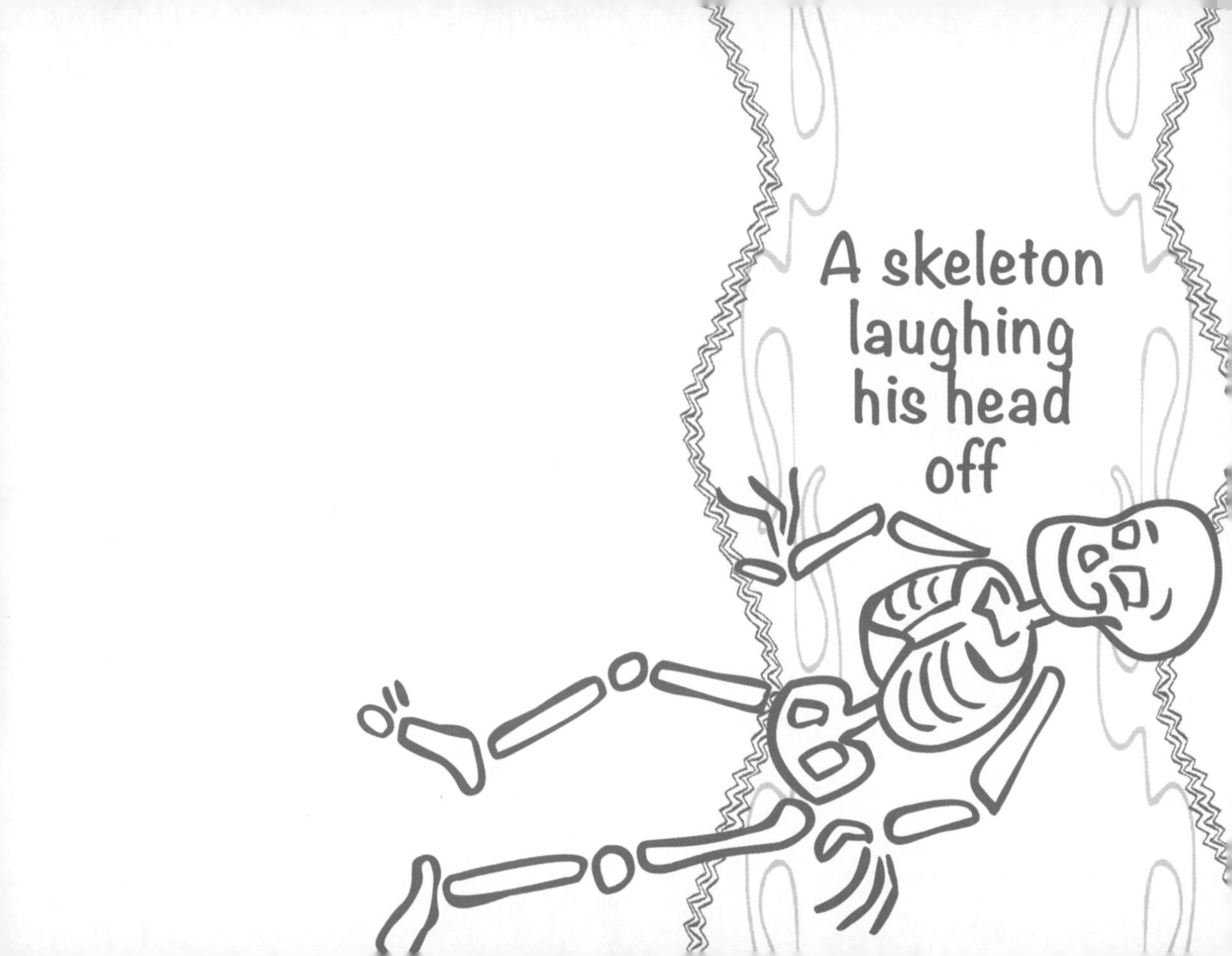
A skeleton laughing his head off

Knock,
knock!
Who's
there?
Boo.
Boo who?

Don't cry,
it's just
a knock-
knock
joke.

Why did the chicken
cross the road?
To buy all the books!
Lunchbox Jokes
978-1-938706-13-4
Lunchbox Jokes:Food
978-1-938706-15-8
Lunchbox Jokes:Animals
978-1-938706-14-1
www.lunchbox-jokes.com
100 Fun Tear-Out Notes for Kids
LunchBox Jokes
Deana Gunn
& Wona Miniati
100 Fun Tear-Out Notes for Kids
LunchBox Jokes
Deana Gunn
& Wona Miniati
Food
100 Fun Tear-Out Notes for Kids
LunchBox Jokes
Deana Gunn
& Wona Miniati
Animals